A TOUCH OF THE CREATURE

Charles Beaumont was born Charles Leroy Nutt in Chicago in 1929. He dropped out of high school in the tenth grade and worked at a number of jobs before selling his first story to *Amazing Stories* in 1950. In 1954 his "Black Country" became the first work of short fiction to appear in *Playboy*, and his classic tale "The Crooked Man" was featured in the same magazine the following year. Beaumont published numerous other short stories in the 1950s, both in mainstream periodicals like *Playboy* and *Esquire* and in science fiction and fantasy magazines.

His first story collection, *The Hunger and Other Stories*, was published in 1957 to immediate acclaim and was followed by two further collections, *Yonder* (1958) and *Night Ride and Other Journeys* (1960). He also published two novels, *Run from the Hunter* (1957, pseudonymously, with John E. Tomerlin), and *The Intruder* (1959).

Beaumont is perhaps best remembered for his work in television, particularly his screenplays for *The Twilight Zone*, for which he wrote several of the most famous episodes. His other screenwriting credits include the scripts for films such as *The Premature Burial* (1962), *Burn, Witch, Burn* (1962), *The Haunted Palace* (1963), and *The Masque of the Red Death* (1964).

When Beaumont was 34, he began to suffer from ill health and developed a baffling and still-unexplained condition that caused him to age at a greatly increased rate, such that at the time of his death at age 38 in 1967, he had the physical appearance of a 95-year-old man. Beaumont was survived by his wife Helen, two daughters, and two sons, one of whom, Christopher, is also a writer.

Beaumont's work was much respected by his colleagues, and he counted Ray Bradbury, Harlan Ellison, Richard Matheson, Robert Bloch, and Roger Corman among his friends and admirers. His work is in the process of being rediscovered with collector's editions of several of his works from Centipede Press, three reissues from Valancourt Books, and a new collection from Penguin Classics.

By Charles Beaumont

COLLECTIONS

The Hunger and Other Stories (1957)★

Yonder (1958)

Night Ride and Other Journeys (1960)

Selected Stories (1988)

A Touch of the Creature (2000)★

NOVELS

Run from the Hunter (1957) (with John E. Tomerlin)

The Intruder (1959)★

NONFICTION

Remember? Remember? (1956) (essays)

Omnibus of Speed (1958) (with William F. Nolan)

★ Available from Valancourt Books

A TOUCH OF THE CREATURE

CHARLES BEAUMONT

with a new introduction by
ROGER ANKER

VALANCOURT BOOKS

First published by Subterranean Press in 2000
First Valancourt Books edition 2015

Copyright © 2000, 2015 by Christopher Beaumont
Introduction copyright © 2015 by Roger Anker

Published by Valancourt Books, Richmond, Virginia
http://www.valancourtbooks.com

ISBN 978-1-941147-98-6
Also available as an electronic book.

All Valancourt Books publications are printed on acid free paper that
meets all ANSI standards for archival quality paper.

Set in Bembo Book MT Pro 10.5/12.6

CONTENTS

INTRODUCTION

The idea for *A Touch of the Creature* first came to Charles Beaumont at the home of Ray Bradbury in August 1953.

At the time, Beaumont was a struggling young writer who had been an ardent devotee of Bradbury's stylish tales of science-fiction since the early Forties—an era that had established Bradbury as a cult favorite among readers of the pulp magazines that were popular in the day.

Born on January 2, 1929, Beaumont had begun reading the pulps in the late Thirties while growing up on Chicago's North Side. Shortly before his twelfth birthday, however, he was stricken with spinal meningitis. While bedridden, he became a fan of authors such as H.G. Wells, Edgar Allan Poe, and L. Frank Baum, creator of the "Wizard of Oz" series of books. "It was he who first showed me what words could do," Beaumont wrote. Midway through his bout of meningitis, Beaumont was sent by his parents to convalesce with his grandmother in Burlington, Washington. It was there that he discovered Bradbury's stories in the pages of *Weird Tales* magazine—stories that fueled his imagination and inspired him to put his own works of fiction on paper. "I love and have always loved to write and to create imaginative word pictures," Beaumont wrote at age fifteen. "I have an extreme interest in grammar and word-construction, and love to read. I believe all these are instrumental in the making of a good author. The only other vocation I could really be happy in is the cousin of fiction writing—playwriting and radio script writing. The deciding factor in all of these is, of course, my intense love of literature."

While Beaumont penned his first stories, he devoted himself to reading the classic works of American literature, becoming an admirer of F. Scott Fitzgerald, William Faulkner, Carson McCullers, James Thurber, and Ernest Hemingway. His personal study of the field indicated how obsessive he could be. By his reasoning, it was not enough to familiarize himself with the critically acclaimed authors, or to be aware of the important, influential literary works; he was driven to know *everything* about the various styles and genres that had cross-pollinated and influenced each other.

During a visit to Los Angeles in the summer of 1946, Beaumont met Ray Bradbury in a downtown bookstore. The two became immediate friends. "We were drawn together by similar tastes and memories," Bradbury said. "We'd both grown up in the Midwest: Chuck in Chicago; me in Waukegan. And even though he was ten years younger than me, he seemed to remember things out of my own boyhood. We shared a love of radio and movies and comics and theater. We loved books and music and *King Kong*. We shared a passion for language. We also missed the changing of the seasons, particularly autumn, the most nostalgic and contemplative of seasons." With so much in common, Bradbury could not help but to encourage young Beaumont as he sought his own career path. "Sometime later, I began critiquing his short stories," Bradbury said. "When I read the first one, I said, 'Yes, very definitely. You are a writer.' It's not like so many people who come to you with stories and you say, 'Well, they're okay; if they keep working they might make it.' Chuck's talent was obvious from that very first story."

Although Beaumont's métier was horror, science fiction, and fantasy, he also turned out numerous works of "mainstream" fiction—stories that spoke of the human condition: "The Rival", like many of his tales of this period, is a story written in a lucid, invigorating style that came to him early in his writing life; "With the Family" is a prime example of a non-plot character story; "Mr. Underhill" is an intriguingly cryptic piece in which Beaumont concludes the story with suggestion rather than overt explanation.

In late 1949, Beaumont married Helen Broun. After the couple moved into a small, two-bedroom apartment in Los Angeles, they converted the spare bedroom into a study. It would be in this monastic room, barely wide enough to hold a desk, but as private as any aspiring writer could hope for—as Helen intended to let her husband work without interruption—that Charles would write a voluminous number of stories that would later establish him as not only one of the top fantasists of his generation, but as a top writer in a variety of fields.

As Beaumont's early fiction brought him little more than rejection slips, he began experimenting with various styles of storytelling. Many of his tales written during this era reveal his remarkable talent for investing ordinary situations with well-crafted characters, bizarre plot twists, and ironic endings. "The Indian Piper" is a beautifully written story of a down-and-out tycoon who is contemplating suicide in a shabby hotel room when he hears the sounds of the strange pipe player emanating from a nearby room. "The Junemoon Spoon" is a tale of rural humor, in which the citizens of a small country town find a way to deal with a dishonest traveling salesman.

Six months after Beaumont and his wife celebrated the birth of their first child, in December 1950, they were introduced to a struggling young writer by the name of Richard Matheson (who, years later, would be known for penning such classics as *I Am Legend*, *The Shrinking Man* and *Somewhere in Time*). As their families became close, there developed between Charles and Richard a constant interchange of ideas, out of which a number of varied and imaginative stories would emerge. "Though Chuck and I never collaborated on a short story, we spent a lot of time discussing the finer points of fiction writing," Matheson said. "We talked about plot, character, style, structure and dialogue." As their careers grew, the pair acted as "spurs" to one another. "He and I—in a very nice way, of course—were very competitive," Matheson said. "At first, I was a little ahead of him in sales. But he caught up to me." Yet, as close as the two of them were as friends, their personalities could not have been more different. "Our stories sort of showed the way we lived and thought," Matheson continued. "I was a homebody. Just a very, almost dull realist. [*Laughs.*] Fortunately, the *ideas* that I've gotten were sort of unusual. But then I would immediately place them in the home situation. The neighborhood situation. Whereas Chuck would get these incredible ideas and they could take place *anywhere* and in any way. He was much more unlimited in his thinking." One such Beaumont tale penned during this period is "Resurrection Island", a cynical story about the film industry written with a pulp slant.

By mid-1953, Beaumont had sold a handful of stories to publications such as *Amazing Stories*, *If: Worlds of Science Fiction*, *Universal-International News*, *Imagination* and *The Magazine of Fantasy and Science Fiction*. Although the promise of additional story sales was on the horizon, he had a family to support. As such, Helen had taken a secretarial position, while Charles worked at a variety of jobs, including that of musical score copier at Universal Studios.

While he spent his nights and weekends penning his tales, he noted that life at the studio had become unbearable, due to "a conflict of interests" with a department supervisor.

When Beaumont was fired in June, he turned to full-time writing.

By August 1953, Beaumont's finances were spiraling out of control. Although Helen's income was sufficient to cover household expenses when her husband's stories were not selling, her family was barely surviving. "Helen understood the tremendous sacrifice that goes into the making of a writer," Matheson said. "The wife of an author must offer her husband hope and encouragement; she needs to be a friend and confidante, a lover, cook and housekeeper; she must possess the patience of a saint. So rather than have Chuck run out and get another job, Helen insisted he stay at the typewriter. She believed in him; believed in his talent."

In late August, Charles and Helen were invited to Ray Bradbury's home for dinner. By now, Bradbury's darkly poetic tales of science fiction and fantasy were challenging readers to explore new horizons. With such acclaimed classics as *The Martian Chronicles*, *The Illustrated Man* and *Fahrenheit 451*, he had introduced social and political themes and asked complex questions that had previously been the territory of serious novelists. Before leaving Bradbury's home, Beaumont learned of the recent offer his host had received from filmmaker John Huston. Bradbury had sent Huston a copy of *The Golden Apples of the Sun*, his recently published collection of short fiction, and was pleased to discover that one of the book's twenty-two stories ("The Fog Horn") had captured the renowned director's attention. As a result, Huston hired Bradbury to adapt Herman Melville's classic novel, *Moby Dick*, for the cinematic screen.

Inspired by Bradbury's good fortune, Beaumont began penning stories around the clock, sleeping an average of four hours a day, surviving on coffee and cigarettes. With a burst of creative energy, he also began putting together his own collection of published and unpublished short fiction. With dozens of stories from which to choose, Beaumont elected to "go with a mainstream and science-fiction package" that would appeal to publishing houses such as Doubleday. After briefly considering several titles, including *A Touch of the Creature*, he decided to call his book *Strange Companions*.

As Beaumont continued to work at a feverish pace, friends and editors noted that his creative and technical writing skills were developing at an astonishing rate. With each new story he redefined his style, and he soon began penning the type of lyrical fiction that would set him apart from other writers.

"Chuck had, I think, as most writers do—but it was exaggerated in Chuck's case—a great desire for recognition, because he had a tremendous ego, which is both a strength and a weakness," recalled John Tomerlin, who had known Beaumont since 1949. "Most, if not *all*, of Chuck's stories involve a character who has some sort of talent or quality that others can't see ... I have a feeling that Chuck felt that way about himself."

In late October, Beaumont learned that Doubleday had rejected *Strange Companions*. "They seemed to feel it wouldn't fit into their science-fiction set-up and that the science-fiction element kept it from their straight list," he wrote. "In short they didn't know how to market the thing." The following month, Beaumont's literary agent submitted a restructured *Strange Companions* to Ballantine Books, who also passed on the manuscript. Undeterred, Beaumont sent a "revamped, multi-genre story package" to Dodd, Mead & Company, after which he and

John Tomerlin decided to collaborate on a short story. "Chuck and I came up with a plot that revolved around a young pregnant woman, hormones, paranoia and despair—in that order!" Tomerlin laughingly recalled. "We called our story 'Moon in Gemini.' Although it never sold, we had fun writing it."

In April 1954, Beaumont's agent received word that *Strange Companions* had been turned down by Dodd Mead: "We've given this manuscript unusual attention because of its remarkable excellence in some respects. Our decision against it came because, first, it is short stories and, second, because the stories don't seem to group together. The title well describes them. If a book of equal distinction could be found with all the stories in the same groove it ought to be a publishing venture. So, reluctantly, the manuscript has been returned to you. If you ever have a full length Beaumont, we'd like to see it, and I think we could make an attractive offer for it."

In response, Beaumont wrote to Dodd Mead: "The 'mixed-bag' idea was an experiment and, apparently, a poor one—at any rate, I have no difficulty sympathizing with your criticism of lack of grouping. It was meant to be 'comprehensive' but ended up being helter-skelter. I am reworking *Strange Companions* . . . I've taken out the science-fiction and humorous stories and substituted other 'straight' stories which I feel represent the very best work of which I am capable. Many of them are brand new, and my personal opinion is that the book will not only be more of a cohesive piece but actually quite superior."

As Beaumont attempted to breathe new life into his collection, the spring of 1955 found him involved in a new and exciting hobby: auto racing. The sport instantly became one of the great fascinations of his life. He soon began to compete in weekend sports car racing events on the West Coast, while writing voluminously for motoring journals such as *Road & Track* and *Sports Cars Illustrated*. His passion for the sport often found its way into his fiction. In his short story, "Fallen Star", his tale opens with its protagonist driving a Porsche Speedster into Palm Springs—a site where Beaumont had raced his own Porsche in sanctioned competition.

By now, Beaumont's stories had begun to appear in the most prestigious magazines in America, including *Esquire*, *The Saturday Evening Post*, *Collier's*, and *Playboy*, for whom he would become a contributing editor. Although his prolific output of fiction and nonfiction embraced a wide variety of moods and genres, Beaumont remained a fantasist at heart. Like Bradbury before him, he helped bring about a sophistication of style and content to the fantasy field. He was a keen observer and social commentator, whose writing exposed the foibles of modern society. Beaumont's stories also reflected his interests and concerns: jazz and music, the dark side of character, the bite of satire.

Upon reading Beaumont's latest works of fiction, Bradbury realized that he had mentored his student well. "Chuck had come into his own," he said. "I instinctively knew there was little more that I could do for him. I felt I'd have only gotten in the way of his natural development if I'd continued to critique his work."

In August 1956, Charles noted that it had been exactly three years since he first launched *Strange Companions*. Since that time, his collection had gone through numerous variations of story line-ups and had been rejected by several publishing houses, including Scribner's and Bobbs-Merrill. "Everyone wanted a novel," Beaumont's agent, Don Congdon, recalled. "But no one wanted short stories in book form." As Beaumont began the search for suitable material for a novel, Congdon learned that Saul David, editorial director for Bantam Books, had expressed interest in publishing *Strange Companions* as a paperback reprint. As a result of David's interest, Congdon contacted Walter Minton of G.P. Putnam's Sons. "He was nervous about putting out a book of short fiction by a virtually unknown author," Congdon said. "At that point, I had no guarantee that Bantam would buy into the collection's paperback rights. So Minton would've been gambling on coming out even on the production expenses of a hardcover edition. But if Bantam came through with the reprint deal, a portion of their money would have gone toward reimbursing Putnam's for some of their expenditure."

In September, Putnam's agreed to publish *Strange Companions*, with the proviso Beaumont change the book's title and amend its lineup of stories. "They were really banking on the Bantam deal coming through," Congdon said, "which, thankfully, it did."

With hardcover and paperback contracts in place, Beaumont continued to turn out short fiction at a prodigious rate. By now, *Playboy* had placed him on a five hundred dollar monthly stipend for first refusal rights to his manuscripts. He had also become a regular contributor to a new men's magazine called *Rogue*, for whom his stories would appear under the pseudonyms "Michael Phillips" and "C.B. Lovehill".

As Beaumont's writing career began its stellar rise, he often found himself juggling several projects simultaneously. "Chuck was always hyper-energetic," Richard Matheson said. "From the time I met him he was *always* restless. Had to move. Had to go someplace. Got to go. I remember him talking about hating the idea of being asleep. He even hated the idea of someone seeing him asleep. Because sleep to him was like: I'm not doing anything. I'm wasting time."

It was with this energy that Beaumont entered into his next project: *The Intruder*, a novel in which he dramatizes the volatile problems of Southern school integration in the 1950s. "I decided to write the book because at last I felt I had a theme that would allow me to do some serious work," Beaumont wrote. "My novel is not entirely fictional ... It concerns itself with a situation that is all too real in America ... Good or bad, the novel does take a stand on the question of integration."

While Beaumont was hard at work on *The Intruder*, his short fiction collection was released in April 1957. Although he had lobbied to have his book retitled *A Touch of the Creature*, he agreed, at Walter Minton's behest, to call the collection *The Hunger and Other Stories*. Named for one of the book's seventeen tales, *The Hunger* drew favorable reviews and enjoyed moderate success in hardcover sales. As such, Bantam decided to publish a second volume of Beaumont's short fiction as a paperback original and scheduled the collection—under the title *Yonder: Stories of Fantasy and Science Fiction*—for an April 1958 release.

By 1959, Beaumont had entered into the world of script-writing for both film and television. But it was on a project uniquely suited to his fantastic imagination that he would receive his widest recognition: *The Twilight Zone*, Rod Serling's seminal, fantasy-based television series. After the show made its network debut, Beaumont became one of its principal writers, penning several of the series's most memorable episodes.

As Beaumont's stories had been providing him with a steady income, he moved his family to another part of Los Angeles, where he had purchased a home. During a chaotic time of expensive renovations throughout early 1960, Charles noted he was pleased to see the release of his third short fiction collection. Although he had once again urged Bantam to name his book *A Touch of the Creature*, the publishing house instead chose the title *Night Ride and Other Journeys*. "One reason for our decision to go ahead with another paperback original had to do with *The Intruder* selling to Putnam's," Saul David recalled. "Another reason was the name recognition Chuck was starting to get from *Playboy* and *Twilight Zone*."

Throughout 1961, Beaumont was at the height of his literary powers, selling to most of the top markets in magazine and television. By now, film offers were also flooding in. At times he juggled as many as ten projects simultaneously.

The following year, however, it seemed as though Beaumont's heavy workload was beginning to take its toll on him. "From the late Fifties into the early Sixties, Chuck was aging at a rate that was extremely rapid," Matheson said. "He was never healthy to begin with; he'd had spinal meningitis as a youth. And for years he suffered from *terrible* migraine headaches. Really awful ones. He *lived* on Bromo Seltzer. He'd buy these huge electric-purple bottles of Bromo and consume them in no time. He was always very, very thin. Almost gaunt. Though he was above six feet in height, he only weighed around one hundred and forty pounds—and that was when he was *healthy*."

The spring of 1963 found Beaumont working on several film, television, fiction and nonfiction projects, while submitting his fourth collection of short fiction to Bantam. The book's lineup of stories included "Time and Again", which concerns parallel deaths in ancient Egypt and modern times, "Lachrymosa", the touching story of a widow and widower meeting in a cemetery; and "Adam's Off Ox", a charming backwoods deal-with-the-devil fantasy that is written in an overtly bucolic style. Once again, Beaumont considered titling his collection *A Touch of the Creature*. Despite lengthy negotiations with Bantam, however, the volume never materialized.

Meanwhile, Beaumont continued his prolific output of stories. Yet for the first time in his career as a professional writer, he found himself struggling with his manuscripts, which saw continuous rewrites, as he was increasingly frustrated with the thoughts and words he was putting to paper. To worsen matters, family and close friends noted that he seemed to be losing the ability to concentrate, the cause of which they attributed to exhaustion from stress and overwork.

In an effort to maintain his status as a writer who was at the peak of his reputation and career, Beaumont continued to struggle through his assignments until he could find time for rest and, hopefully, recovery. Yet, as his concentration worsened, Helen desperately tried to understand and treat his symptoms.

In the summer of 1964, after a battery of tests at UCLA, Charles Beaumont was diagnosed as having either Alzheimer's disease or Pick's disease, both of which are degenerative disorders of the brain and are recognized by doctors only through an autopsy. As each disease is largely untreatable and totally incurable, Beaumont faced premature senility, aging, and an early death.

The following year, Beaumont was taken to the Motion Picture Country Home and Hospital in Woodland Hills, California.

He died there on February 21, 1967 at the age of thirty-eight, his full potential never realized.

★   ★   ★

Charles Beaumont's favored title was finally realized in 2000 when *A Touch of the Creature* was published in two hardcover formats: a numbered edition that featured fourteen previously unpublished stories, and a lettered edition that included three additional previously unpublished tales ("The Philosophy of Murder", "The End Product," and "The Blind Lady"). Now, with the release of Valancourt Books' paperback edition of *A Touch of the Creature*, all seventeen stories are collected in this volume.

Like the best of Beaumont's work, the tales within bridge the gap between pre-World War II and modern styles of storytelling. However, the innovations he and his colleagues brought to fantasy and horror are the foundations of those genres' current popularity. As such, every writer, artist, or filmmaker who has followed Beaumont into that night country he knew so well owes him an enormous debt.

Upon reading these stories for the first time—decades after Beaumont's passing—Richard Matheson noted that the tales in this collection had been a revelation to him: "All these years … I was under the impression that I had a clear picture of Chuck. I thought I had read all his work. I thought I had an accurate fix on his plotting, stylistic and character delineating skills. And certainly his persona.

"Obviously, I was wrong."

Matheson was particularly struck by the intellectual and emotional impact of "The Pool", a tale that concerns the frustrations of a young professional writer and family man. "Chuck was, literally, able to get inside himself, a feat only the best writers (or any superlative artist) can achieve," Matheson wrote. "Nor, apparently, did he fear that inward probe and unflinching self-study which he was able to translate into words.

"In this particular story, what more perfect evocation could be created for a writer wanting to yet unable to resist the largesse of writing scripts. A problem complicated by the responsibilities of marriage and parenthood. On a personal level, Chuck dealt with all of this.

"This sorrow is familiar to me as it would be to any writer who yearns to write something truly important but lives in a state of constant frustration because he doesn't.

"With Chuck, there was further complication to this problem—a complication he was not aware of—his demise at the maddening age of 38.

"Knowing all this, 'The Pool' is, to me in particular, a work of deep—and horrific—import."

Matheson also noted that he had been "thrown off-balance" by the other stories in this volume, all of which had been a "revelation" to him: "One which I did not expect. One which unsettled me. But one I am happy to have experienced. How often in life, after such a long period of years, is one struck by such a revelation?

"Especially regarding an old friend and creative companion who, one discovers, was far different—and far *larger*—than one ever thought he was."

Roger Anker
July 8, 2015

Roger Anker is a Bram Stoker Award-winning editor, and he has also written for numerous magazines, including *Twilight Zone*, *Starlog*, *Fangoria*, *Fantasy Review*, *Dark Discoveries*, and *Mystery Scene*. He lives in Chicago, where he is currently writing *Trapped in the Twilight Zone: The Life and Times of Charles Beaumont* for Centipede Press.

Adam's Off Ox

Hesh! The Good Lord in Judgment, get down there; you'ns must not crawl all over me like the scurvy. Swear, think after a body's worked hard all day—*let go a that brooch or I'll whup you to within a ace of your life!*—think a body could expect a little rightful rest. And you needn't act smart nor cute neither, because it don't fool me for one solitary minute: I have paid particular heed how that when they is beans to be popped and taters to peel you could ruin the muscles of your neck lookin for help, but once the work is all tended to—*little old feisty crawly things, get down before you break both my legs!* I'll be witness, you're all busier than a cow's tail in fly time; and here it is long beyont reasonable bed-time.

Now what ails you?

Nosir. It is altogether too late to be startin in on a big old long drawn-out story.

And *I* say it is, and we'll hear no more of it.

Besides, I have told you all the histories I could study up, and then some.

Hesh!

All right, all *right*. But listen to me: Do you'ns solemnly swear and give your oath that when I'm done you'll march into bed and not another word out a you?

Is that a solemn swear?

Then stop dodaddlin around; quit your old fussin; and clear the phlegm out a your throats.

And get down off me!

Now then.

Reckon I've already spelled out the story of my Great Uncle Billy Spiker and How He Met up with The Devil hisself in the Woods and like to Died at What Happent When He was Give that One Wish . . .

No?

Wellsir:

My Great Uncle Billy Spiker was a caution. He growed up like any normal child, and was give all the advantages a mother's lovin heart could provide, but his daddy was a heller and wanted Billy to enter the trappin business but Bill was a mind not to and that's when he lit out. Aged fourteen at the time; and nobody heard hide nor tail of him agin.

Entered a good many lines of business, Billy did, but he never could seem to stick at nothin—stay a while and the man he worked for, they'd hold him up like their own kin; then somebody would pass the corn liquor and Great Uncle would go off somewheres and stay three, four weeks. And that would be the end of that. He'd get jobs and lose em, get em and lose em, allers lookin for somethin, I guess, like—nobody ever could rightly understand, he was so peculiar.

Wellsir, he might have got liquored up, and maybe he wasn't no count in a lot of respects, but he's one man who never made a real enemy. Not a real one.

This, you must understand, is all before he begun callin hisself Doctor Marvel-O.

That came about in a peculiar way. My Great Uncle was remarked in a good many states for his way with the cards. Lot a folks recomembered how he used to swagger into some barroom or other and smile a smile that'd charm a coon right out of a tree, smile and set down and, be blamed, he'd make total paupers a half the men in that room before you could say scatwallix. Most other men would a got shot up sure as sin, but old Billy took their money ever time and left em laughin at their own cussed luck.

Wellsir, it so happent one time, when the tide was turned around for a spell and he was nigh to bedrock, that he got involved in a game a poker. Things went along just fine and dandy and Billy was winnin away, when a certain gentleman owned up that he didn't have any more money but he would bet all his other worldly possessions on that last hand, if my Great Uncle would do the same.

Now Billy he couldn't see but one thing to do. Says, "Hellfire yes!" and they drawed.

And Billy won.

And here is what he won: A big old creaky wagon, a thousand empty bottles, a horse a hundred years old or so named Queen Elizabeth III and a colored gentleman without no teeth and sad eyes named Ephriam-Ephriam X. And a banjo.

Don't you know Billy laughed fit to be tied when he seen his winnins. But he had a queer sort a wisdom and he made his decision right then and there.

They was sign on the wagon read:

DOCTOR MARVEL-O'S
A PANACEA FOR ALL AILMENTS
A YOUTH REVIVIFIER
AND!!
GUARANTEED TO INCREASE YOUR GROWTH
ONLY $1.00 A BOTTLE

So then he bought a black suit with a white shirt and spectacles; and from the start he made an insistence that Ephriam-Ephriam had to address him as Doctor.

Hiked up and begun to travel then, once he'd mixed up a batch a medicine. You understand, of course, he did this all hisself: throwed water and all kinds of things, like sassafras root, clover weed and molasses, into a big tub a corn whisky and stirred her all up.

Did I mention he was a borned talker? Hey-O; probably knew more about words than anybody else to begin with, so when he come to the first town in his yeller wagon, and after Ephriam-Ephriam got through strummin out melodies, it were no wonder he sold ever full bottle he had.

And that is the way she went. From town to town, year in and year out, Doctor Marvel-O just went on mixin up his potions in the tub and lyin like a jackrabbit all the time to folks to get em to buy his Miracle Mix. Shoo-*eee*, how that man did frebaricade!

But it never done nobody any real harm, exceptin them as

imbibed too much and got the naushy due to the corn whisky taste. Didn't do em any good, though, neither: not one last drap a good; and that's what got ta jabbin Great Uncle Billy till he couldn't sleep right of a night anymore.

They was both out in this here part a the country—a long time fore even I was thought of—when Billy got to studyin things, and fell into a black old mood. The wagon was stuck in a mud puddle smack the middle of a forest, and for a long time they sat there, whilst it poured down rain outside, and finally Billy said: "Hit don't seem right that a man should go on through life without doin a single solitary thing for nobody. Don't seem right, no matter how you look at her."

He didn't know how much his cussed smile had ever meant to more pretty janes than I got toes, or how many folks felt better just by listenin to him lie.

Ephriam-Ephriam practically never talked, so he just listened. Nobody knows what he thought about it all.

I say Great Uncle Billy set and studied, whilst it rained, then he started shakin his head like to come loose from his shoulder-blades. And then he weeped, for the first time in his whole adult life and it was a powerful thing to behold, as he thunk about all them years and how he'd be a parson or a doctor—a *real* doctor —if it was to do over agin.

Wellsir, Ephriam-Ephriam took out his banjo and hummed a spiritual song. They'd have to wait for the rain to quit and things to dry anyway fore they could come unstuck, so Billy heshed his cryin and crawled inta the back a the wagon and begun to mix up another batch a mednis.

First, though, he tried out the corn liquor to see that it was of the usual high quality, no doubt. Tried her out agin, he did, and got to think about how dog miserable he was and all, and he kep on tryin out that whisky until they wasn't a overgenerous amount left when he got through.

But hit helped his mood out. Got to singin and whoopin and hollerin, like to out-shout that old storm hitself; and then, Great Uncle Billy Spiker started gatherin up things for his Miracle Mix.

He threw in ever last thing he could lay his hands to. Lamp

oil, kerosene, rusted nails, handkerchiefs, old love letters from women he liked at first didn't later on when they begun to love him up too much, week-old socks—Billy just kep on tossin things inta that old tub. Soon it begun to bubble and bile and spit, but the more noise it made the louder Billy sung and it appeared as if he was goin to put old Ephriam-Ephriam X in too, ony he was too heavy.

"Double double toil an trouble," Billy shrieks out.

O, twas weird. Queen Elizabeth III got worried and fretted feisty-like: come nigh rearin up.

Then—well now, here is where the interestin part comes in.

After that tub got ta jumpin with all the peculiar things Billy had throwed inside, Billy he took him a notion to go walkin.

So he clumb out the wagon and like to lit on his head in the mud, he was so saturated, but he dint. Made her all right and laughed like a hyeeny, he did, at the pitisul sight of that yeller rig and the old hoss and Ephriam-Ephriam settin big and proud in the pourin down rain, spang in the midst of them Skagit woods.

Begun to walk and seein as how they wasn't no more spirits, he got to thinkin agin and there he was, thrice as miserable as a body can get.

Fore long he was out of sight of the wagon and anything else human—just walkin in the rain, stumblin and fallen all over hisself like a man gone demented, tryin to study, don't you understand what I'm sayin, tryin to kindy sort and figure and study it all out and see what the sum come to.

Now, a course, they is every good chance that what took place then was a total dream all in my Great Uncle Billy's head, which was whirlin and spinnin to Glory due to the corn whisky. But them as has lived out some years, they get to know the difference betwixt an between dreams and real-to-life occurrences. Leastways, I will tell it to go it come about as actual, and if you'ns choose to say Billy Spiker was just dead old drunk and not accountable, then you are as welcome as the air to do so.

Well now, don't you know it vexed Billy when, as he elected to sit down on a old log and listen to the rainy wind, there come big and loud a hee-haw and a hee-haw louder'n a mule's bray!

He jumped up and looked around for a good stick, and then he caught a glimmer of who it was was doin all that laughin and it struck God's own fear into my Great Uncle's heart.

Now mind, he were no coward. Billy had fought him many's the good old fight, includin Apache injuns and men twicet his size and geirth, and he was never knowed to be a shirker.

But he took one look at who was laughin his fool head off, and he said: "Feet, let us go!" But those old feet, they was rooted to the ground and preliminated movement of any kind, shade or description. Billy begun to tremble like a aspirin.

"It is certainly wet out," says Billy, poochin out his chest.

"Don't take much sense to see that, now does it?" says the other, comin closer.

"I was tryin," says Billy, "to be sociable."

And upon that, this here old man—gettin closer all the time —he laid his head back and laughed and sniggered till you'd think he'd choke.

He was a study, let me tell you all. A big man it was, standin there laughin at Billy Spiker—big and ornry lookin and by no stretch of the imagination just exactly right. For one thing, he didn't have no hair on his whole body, and you could say this for a fact because the old vulgarian was naked as a jaybird, without even nothin to cover his modesty! Head slicker'n a bean and flatter on the top than two pancakes. Also, he was jetty black—just as black old black as the ace of spades. Not like Ephriam-Ephriam X, I don't mean, but—well, like a lump a hard coal: shiny and wet, as if he'd been scorched in the fire for a long time so's it turned from red to black and the scars blistered all over. When he smiled, you could see his little sharp pointy teeth set in a row, and his bitty eyes, like a fish's eyes, ony a deep bright bloody red.

But the most uncommon thing about him was the fact that right smack on his temples was two horns—ram's horns.

Also he breathed out breath that stunk a lime and brimstone and switched his old tail around like a snake in a cesspool.

Can you see now why Great Uncle Billy was uncomftable?

Or maybe you wouldn't be, you'ns is so brave—there late of a night, with Lucifer in the flesh breathin his hot breath on you!

"Hi!" says Billy finally, cause the drink it does do one thing: it does take away that old yeller streak up a man's backside. "Hi! Looks as how they's a couple of us here lackin in sense. Else why would Satan be roamin these wet woods without no clothes on, shiverin and chatterin, stead a perched up on his nice warm throne in Hades?"

Satan quit a hee-hawin, scratched at his head, then begun to laugh all the harder.

Well now, this begun to get on Billy's nerves. He was feelin a cold comin on, anyway, so he stomped his foot and said, "Hesh up! You're enough to give a body the jumps with your infernal cacklin."

Satan, he let out a big old belch, and scrooched down so's to be more of a level with Great Uncle.

"Kind a sassy," says he, "for a mere human, it do seem to me."

And all this time, you understand, Billy couldn't dast to move a budge.

"I pre*sume*," says Billy—I mentioned he had the tongue?—"I pre*sume* I am being waylaid here for a better reason than to catch my death a pneumonee."

"Hee haw," says Satan; then he looked down slantwise, breathin out that brimstone. "Listen here to me, William Jacob Spiker—" He knowed Great Uncle Billy's full Christian name, which was a genuine revelation in itself. "—if they's anythin I mortally loathe and despise, it's a man that wants somethin good and bad but don't have the gumption to fess it up."

"I'm mighty afraid I don't foller you."

"Ah, but *I* have follered *you*, William Jacob Spiker; all the way from Coopersville, when you first developed this here unhappiness you got lodged tight in your bosom. Been a waitin for you to call uponst me, waitin patient, but . . . well, blame it, hit's *cold* out here!"

Satan give a shiver that like to knocked his eyeteeth out a his livin head.

"Well now," says Great Uncle Billy, givin particular heed to the situation as best he could when you consider the corn whisky. "I imagine you *are* a mite chilly at that. My house is a poor one, stuck in the mud ta boot, but whatever warmth is there, she's as welcome as the flowers in May to your use."

Satan grinned and lit a big black cigar with the tip of his tail. "Very well," says he, "I accept your invitation. I always talk better in front of a good fire anyhow."

So they tromped back through them old woods to the wagon and clumb on in thout disturbin Ephriam-Ephriam or Queen Elizabeth III. Oncet inside, Satan begun to rub his hands together and Great Uncle Billy was fair disturbed to note how black his visitor was in the lamplight—black and bad-evil lookin, but also kind a sad.

Wellsir, when old King Lucifer had thawed hisself out, and stretched and lazied around, he said: "What I meant was, knowin you and your histry, I figured that sooner or later you'd be callin on me."

Things was screwjeed and whirlin in Billy's mind—I told you that. Under what a body'd call normal circumstances he was a smart man, but now—well, he filled him two cups with corn soakins, give one to the Devil and they drunk a solemn toast.

Says Billy: "I am a unhappy man."

"Ahhh," says Satan.

"Miserable dog lonely; whole dang life wasted, without a single solitary thing to show for it that I was ever on Earth!" says Billy.

Says Satan: "Ahhhh." He gulped his liquor and they got down to business.

"I wish—" Billy starts out to say. Satan, he whupped out a pad a asbestosy stuff and wet the point a his tail, which also served as a pencil.

"William Jacob Spiker," says he, "I presume you know the rules? I grant you one wish, whatsoamever it may be—within reason—and in exchange, I get your everlastin soul. You know all about that?"

Great Uncle Billy took him another swaller and nodded his head slowly.

"Just a formality," says the Devil. "Always have to make sure, else it don't work to my benefit." Then he sneezed out a fiery sneeze that spread pieces a hot coal and cinder like they was germs.

"What is your wish?" says Satan, honkin his nose.

"Wellsir, your honor," answers Billy, "it don't require much thought at that. See here: For years I have been traipsin hither and yon, hither and yon, tellin folks all over the country all about my Miracle Mix and as how it'll grow hair on a bunion and make em tall and strong and improve their complexion, and ekcetera—"

"I been watchin you," quoth Satan, "with high approval." He sniffled up one side a his nose and got his hind end up as close to the lamps as he could.

"Lies; untruths; falsehoods; and nothin else *but*—most a my growed adult life, come to nought. Nought, hear?"

They drunk them another cup a corn.

"Listen here to me," says my Great Uncle. "You can take my old soul and play with it to your heart's content—"

"If—" interrupts Satan, grinnin like a horse.

"If . . . you let me be tellin the truth just once. Lied all my days; now let it come to pass ever word I speak is a word a solemn fact. Just *one* time; that's all I ask: just *one* time."

"I know what you got in your head, William Jacob: a highly evil thought."

"I reckon so."

"Well now, that's fine. Granted." Satan smacked his black old lips and the drool, which was hot lava, come down his chin.

Billy rumbled out a sigh and settled back.

They sat listenin to the rain for a spell.

"Ony one thing worries me," says Billy.

"Ask away, boy."

"Well, what I want to know is, just what do you want to be goin around collectin up people's souls *for*, anyhow?"

"Ridiculous question, boy."

"I mean, what earthly good is a soul?"

Satan, he like ta ruint his jowls smilin. "No *earthly* good at all."

"Well, but—what do you *do* with em?" Billy looked really

perplexed. "I ask solely for information," says he, "seein our business is closed, so to speak."

Satan sipped at his liquor and scrooged up his face. "This here is a highly unusual conversation," says he. "Hmm. You want ta know what I *do* with souls, hey? Let's see now: give me a minute ta study ... Hmm. You mean, what do I *do* with— Well, I— That is— Hellfire, what's in this corn anyways? Danged if I can recomember; though I know well they is *some* reason."

"Must be," says Great Uncle Billy, "cause you sure work yourself into a sweat to get em. Well, she'll come to you; meantime, have another snort."

The rain had stopped now, but they didn't appear to notice. Billy thought it would be best to treat the Devil civil, so they swapped stories and told riddles and before you know it, they was both flopped down on the floor of the wagon, breathin out that vile old alky breath and snorin twicet to the dozen.

Ephriam-Ephriam X found Great Uncle Billy the nex mornin, and let me tell you, he did have a time withal, cause Billy was all owly-eyed and had a head two and a half sizes bigger'n a punkin. Wellsir, they worked the wagon out a that mud and went on through the woods and it weren't till they come to this little town name of Mt. Slocum, which is now the fish hatchery nigh Camano Island, that Billy recomembered. Then it all come back, fuzzy-like—not as twere a dream, you understand, but like as how it didn't actually happen except in his mind.

His head was hurtin and his tongue felt like the entire Union army had marched over it barefoot; so he just sat sullen and surly and permitted Ephriam-Ephriam to make all the arrangements: bottle the new batch a mix, and ekcetera.

He didn't remember most a the conversation with the Old Black Man, except they was the notion he had played host to the Devil hisself, which seemed a sorry joke.

Now then, I want you'ns ta know that this here was fur trappin land. Mt. Slocum was a bitty place, but a fair town in them days: had its general store and cabaret and even a Catholic church, unless that is a false rumor. Lot a people there, anyhow, doin good business and makin money hand over fist. And all around em, big forests drenchy green with the wet and smellin a thick spruce and fir. Hi law, twas beautiful country then.

Now Dr. Marvel-O—Great Uncle Billy—rested on his tailbone till he felt summit better—leastways in body, for it begun to look as how this mood was a permanence—then, he took him on a fresh load a corn liquor—he was a drinkin man and drinkin men just don't ever learn—and he pitched tent.

Then he waited till noontime; and begun to beat on his African Ectasy Drum, which was in reality a slop jar painted over with Crow symbols.

"Hey-O! Hi! Hi! Hooo-eee!" he shouted, "Gather ye round, Hooo-*eee!*"

As per usual, the folks begun to cluster all around, ta see who twas was makin such a all-fired racket. Then, when they was clumped up tight, Ephriam-Ephriam strutted out in his yeller and red and green silk finery and sung a parcel a songs, mostly glad songs, pickin that banjo faster nor a hummin bird's wings.

When he was done, and that crowd was worked up ta fever pitch, then Great Uncle Billy stepped forrards and delivered his speech.

Great, great, how that man could talk! Angels couldn't sing no sweeter about the Pastures a Heaven than he did about Dr. Marvel-O's Miracle Mixture. Them words, I tell ya, lost all connection with anythin real, and he bout like ta spoke in tongues! Quoted, Billy did: the Bible—both Testaments—Shakespeare, poetry; the words come flyin out in the cold air and melted everybody down; flew and danced and jumped, all about how they was no moral reason for a man ta be run down and sickly and short and bald and important—no reason in the world, nosir, not when they was Dr. Marvel-O's Mixture to be had, and for ony a dollar a full bottle.

Don't you know, they was champin at the bit to buy—all the little old bitty runts and pipsqueaks and mealy-mouthed puds in the whole blamed town!

In a mite, the bottles was all gone: sold, ever one.

Well, old Ephriam-Ephriam waited for the crowd ta go away, then he put the things together and they was prepared to move on. (Hit weren't such a good idea to stay around long afterwards, for reasons you can guess.)

"What's this?" says Great Uncle Billy, oncet they was movin. "Eph, looky here."

Twas a single bottle of the mix, settin all ta itself on the stand —and full up ta brimmin.

"Huh," says Ephriam-Ephriam.

"Thought we sold em all," says Billy, rubbin his chin. "Could a swore we did."

Didn't seem any more ta say about that old bottle, so they kep movin and in a little ways they was back in the woods agin.

And Billy got ta thinkin agin. "Nother town, nother pack a bald-faced lies," says he. "I don't know, Eph: I just don't know."

She got inky dark. And the stars begun ta twinkle up high in the heavens, what you see between the treetops.

And even if he would a tried, Great Uncle Billy Spiker couldn't a felt no worse.

And that's the way it went, for a spell. Then:

"Hoooeee! Lordy!" Twas Ephriam-Ephriam, in one a his rare talkin moods."Hit's a h'ant!" says he.

Billy blinked at his eyes, and peered out inta the dusk.

Now then, don't you know that—mebbe two mile out a Mt. Slocum—along come this peculiar figure, just a creepin through the wood towards the wagon.

"Goddy!" says Great Uncle, jumpin up, cause this creature they spied was enough to scare a body within a ace a their lives.

And on hit come, like a regular old ghost, but turned out not ta be a h'ant, somever, but a bona fide honest man. Let me remark, they was a sigh a relief heard right along about then.

"Howdy," says Billy, when the man come within hailin distance. "Youghrtn't a skulkyfoot around thataway: been somebody else would a been plumb skeert."

"Ha ha," says the Stranger; and Billy could a bit off his tongue for speakin thus.

Now this'rn was a sight. Lean old sick scrawny: without the question, the weakest little dried-up whitey peachpit of a man either of em ever did lay eyes on to. Walked with two pine-wood canes, he did, and Billy swore that when he turn't sidewise they wasn't no detectin' him at *all*. White as a sheet, grinnin out a bloodless thin old lips; but he had good eyes, good eyes he had, and when Ephriam-Ephriam X seen them, he unlaxed his holt on the quirt—with the help a which he had been aimin ta snatch that spook bald-headed at the first move.

"Ha ha," says the Stranger. "I'm mighty sorry—can see where *I* would skeer anybody thout warnin. But I live close ta here and was just comin home from town."

Good eyes and sad, had he, and they was strange ta behold setting straight in that pasty face a hisn. He weren't no more than four feet high—did I mention?

Says Billy, "Good old ways to travel by foot, ain't she?"

"Body gets used to it, I reckon," quoth the Stranger.

"Your diggins up the road?"

"Nigh a mile, bit off the fork."

"Well now, seems to me I receive a augury a storm," says Billy, hunchin down his head and lookin at Ephriam-Ephriam. "Since we'ns is travelin that way anyhow, it don't seem right to me that a body ought ta have ta walk."

The Stranger made a examination a Billy's face, then he says: "Thank you kindly," and begun ta squirm and cripple his way to the seat. Great Uncle Billy give it some thought and decided he'd best lend a hand, or else that little feller would a plummeted sure.

"A quaff ta cut the evenin chill?" says Billy, oncet they was movin agin, but hit don't behoove the Stranger. He ony set up straight as he could, answerin civil questions civil, but not in-clined to talk a great deal.

Billy got out the jug, begged pardon and took him a good old pull. "Ahhh," says he.

But somethin begun to get him about this feller. Twas actu-ally a youngster, compared to Billy and Billy thought like this:

Lord God; here's a picture! Two brothers if ever they was. That one gnarlied-up and wasted and ugly as a billy goat on the outside, but young and full up with years; this one gnarlied-up and wasted and ugly as a billy goat on the inside, but with all them years layin in the muck ahint. Lord God, thought Billy, wishin' he could spell it out for the Stranger so's ta make hisself clear: We're two peas in a pod, but between the two which is ta be sought? And which ta despise?

He took on spirits *for* the spirits; which was a favorite joke of his.

So him, duded out in the soily black suit and specs a pure glass, him: DR. MARVEL-O, Great Uncle Billy, old and sad; Ephriam-Ephriam X, rottin out and decayed and still breathin when by rights he should a been to his Reward long afore; and this Stranger, this crippled boy—did I say anythin about that hump on his back standin out the size of a melon?—they rode along in the night.

Then they come to this fork, and the Stranger says: "This here goes off ta my house." He waited, stumblin and stutterin in his speech. "Err," says he, "Ah, gentlemen—may I—" Blushed right pink, that boy. "That is, would you'ns care for a dip, a snoose and a little tea, maybe—course, they's nothin to keep you from sayin no."

Billy gazed inta them big blue-green eyes and thought he had never seen anythin so all-fired sad: right old pleadin sad, as if it had taken the boy clear till now ta summon up the question.

"Wellsir now, you know," says Billy, "we'd be delighted." And they turned that old wagon off the fork and went over holes and ruts like to bounced em ta Kingdom Come and back. Then they drawed nigh a rickety-rackety old shack looked more like a out-house nor a home—clean and all; but tumbled down, without no one ta fix her up.

When they got inside, old Ephriam-Ephriam pronounced: "Heyuuu Lord a mighty!"

Do you know what was in there, spang in the midst a the floor? A ox.

A lean old starved-out shanky ox, squatted down in that room just as proud as you please, whupping that old tongue around so lazified, as sleepy and content as a hound dog. And twicet as much to home.

Billy squinted his eyes at Ephriam-Ephriam for him ta hesh up and settle down: poor Eph, he allers took a fright at somethin queer or not right as it should be; and from his point a view, a ox in the livin room were not right as it should be.

The Stranger looked sad. "Go on out," he says, slow and embarrassy, "they's compny tonight."

And upon the Sainted Name—believe I'll take a swear at this —that dumb animal, without that much brains, without the gumption of a cat, hit riz up like hit understood ever word and walked on out.

The Stranger, he got all glary eyed and sore like all of a sudden. Mostly he directed the venom of his spleen towards Ephriam-Ephriam, sayin:

"Make your fun, go on and make it. I spose the sight of a ox inside a house is a literal scream to you'ns. But I say, a body got to have at least *one* friend. Don't matter none who nor what, long as it's a *friend*!"

Billy got him out a elder toothbrush that he'd made, and dipped inta the snoose and found that twas good snoose.

"Mighty good," he says ta the boy; but hit didn't cut off his screechins.

"You'ns is the first ones been in here to visit me in goin on two year; I swear that to the Holy God!"

Great Uncle Billy, he understood. Didn't know why; but they just didn't seem to be anythin this boy could tell further about hisself that's be surprisin.

"I'm—sorry," says the boy, wringin his hands and lookin ashamed. "It's been up at the crack and inta Mt. Slocum and then odd-job woman's work for me; and folks don't—well, they don't understand. I shouldn't a asked you'ns here: don't rightly know how to act—but I did oncet! Yes I did! If ony I could re-comember . . . Use to be strong, would you believe me: could do two men's work, afore; and folks come to visit me. They come to visit me, and we'd play games and wrassle and just set and study . . . Course I allers had this hump, but hit never made me weakly and people disregarded the blame thing." The boy begun to pace, like, hoppin around and around the floor. "Then I taken sick . . . wellsir, I may look funny ta you now, but I'm tryin to say, they was a day I did my share."

Billy just looked on, not knowin what ta say; or else, knowin they really wasn't nothin *to* say.

Says the boy: "Set up there at Jeremy Boaz and ordered me my earned nips with the best of em, then——stead a froggin around, turnin everybody's stomach, beggin ta wash laundry, beggin ta sew dresses, beggin ta stay alive. And what *for* is a problem I do ponder."

"Tea's bilin," hollers Ephriam-Ephriam. The boy shook his head and said him nary another word about hisself. Twas like he'd had him a good enema; but he didn't look no happier nor a body does after one a those consarned things: ony he got hit out a his system and set back ta wait for her ta build up agin.

Twas after the tea, pipin hot and good to the taste, that Great Uncle Billy Spiker begun to put things together. He thunk him up a reglar army a thoughts, whilst they set around and this crippled boy fought ta keep from cryin.

Then: "Hit's Destiny!" hoots out Billy, snappin his fingers, spillin the tea and grinnin exactly like a sheep. "Destiny hit is as sure as I'm settin here, sure as they is trees outside and clouds of a evenin. The Destiny of Fate!"

Ephriam-Ephriam X had fallen sound asleep, which habit he was in the custom a doin whenever he didn't feel right ta home in a place.

"Hallelujah!" Billy bellered; then he skedaddled outside, sayin to the crippled boy "Don't you go way, now." He went out ta the wagon and scooped up that there bottle a mix, the one as was left over you will please recall, and quoth in a whisper:

"Satan? You hear me, Satan?"

There comes a big old blast a warm air skutterin along the ground, whuppin at his legs. Billy smiled him a smile and held on ta that bottle. Says he: "If you were no dream," addressin the empty air out by the kindlin box, "Say, if you were no dream, and you be true ta your word, then listen here: Am I about ta tell the truth? Is what I say goin ta be legal bindin, gospel true, about this here?" He lifted the bottle.

Come the answer, low and warm.

Billy sighed.

"That's all I wanted ta know," says he, and back inta the house he went.

Ephriam-Ephriam had woke up and was watchin Billy out in the yard, you see, talkin to hisself; his old eyes was bugged out fair ta poppin. But, a course, he said nought.

The young Stranger was pouched in a corner on a stool, stirrin at his tea, lookin misery in the face.

Billy smiled and held out the bottle with its label: DR. MARVEL-O'S MIRACLE MIXTURE; smiled agin, and commenced his spiel.

Now, you couldn't rightly call them words as come out. Not words as you and me use em, although words they *was* and nothin else. But, don't you see, that was just part of it. Twas the tone and pitch, and the way he rolled his eyes that put meat in them words and made em shake and quiver and blow up with truth. Even Ephriam-Ephriam set there all atrancey. You may imagine the effect on the young Stranger.

"Within this phial," says Billy, "is a amalgam; decocted by personal research on private papers containin three hundred years' accumulated study. When I unleashed my discovry upon the world, I was overwhelmed with fabulous offers of such tre-mendous size as ta reel the senses. Could a sold her to ever hospital in the country, but they would a shushed hit up cause Dr. Marvel-O's Miracle Mixture would a put all the doctors out a jobs. So I kep the secret formula and decided to tour the land and let all the people receive the benefits a my mednis, at a price they could afford—" Ekcetera, ekcetera he went on, tellin about the mix; how they was nothin, no sickness nor malady nor affliction hit wouldn't cure right away; how it'd make a man grow big and tall; how it'd make him strong and the envy a others for his physique. Great Uncle Billy got wound up, and must a spieled on about that old stuff nigh a hour.

When he finished, he give her a flourish and set the bottle down on the table.

Now, the young Stranger was lookin confused and kiny hurt. Says: "This here is a terrible cruel joke for you'ns ta be pullin on me."

Ephriam-Ephriam's mouth hung open wide, and they was reproof and nonbelief writ across his features. He had never knowed The Doctor ta do a conscious cruel thing to nobody.

"My boy," says Billy, really worked up, "what I have told you is the truth, the whole truth and nothin else but. You take on a bottle, see if I ain't tellin you right."

The boy made a sour face. "You tryin to tell me that this old greeny stuff'll make me feel better?"

"Feel better is the understatement a the age," says Billy. "Boy, ain't you been listenin ta me?"

"Mean that what's in that there bottle?" says the boy.

"Yessireebob," says Billy.

"That old stuff?"

Billy, he laughed and smiled and hee-hawed; and Ephriam-Ephriam was ever bit a wondrous. Wondrous was Ephriam-Ephriam.

"Well," says the boy, hesitatin; then he says: "Schytte, fire and egg shells! They ain't no sense at all to this whole thing. Sides which, I heard your talk back in Mt. Slocum, and I don't have any more money now nor I did then; no money for nothin, let alone old patent mednis."

To which Bill pipes up: "So happens, friend, that this here is a free sample. Now mind: the taste is piert, but don't you dare take it cept all at once."

Great Uncle Billy Spiker was a big, nice lookin man. Says: "Go on; take it myself, I do!" He was mighty persuasive.

This poor boy, squatted there like a monkey thout its feathers, didn't ere dast to waxen aught but the uttermost respect.

"Furthermore," says Billy, workin at the cork, "it acts as a laxity and cure for the gallopin skitters and other simular ailments."

He was passin it on over to that skeert boy quakin in his boots there, when this here old ox I mentioned come amoseyin back in.

"Hiyeee Goddy!" says Ephriam-Ephriam X, like: What in the good, green earth is goin ta happen next?

Though it must be said that that young feller didn't seem over sad ta see that old critter. He accepted the bottle was bein pressed onta him.

"Throw her on down," says Billy, feelin that warm draft agin his legs.

Feller was right nervous, though, like he had holt a some kind a pizen. "Err, sh," says he, scaloochin and hoppin over to the livestock, "would hit, you think mebbe, this here mednis—you reckon would hit work on Babe here?"

"Hmmm," says Billy, thoughtful, but this wasn't hardly the place to bring up the question with Satan, so he give a guess. "Wellsir, they say a ox's belly is not dissimular to a human's in its revolutions, so I'd say—yes, I reckon the Miracle Mix would do all right with her."

Young feller give a breath a relief and hobbled over to that scrawny old ox. "Here now, Babe," says he, trembly, spoonin out a drap a the tonic inta a big soup ladle. That animal looked fair starved, the skin loopin and fallin over the bones—more like a hat rack than a ox, if you'ns want to know the truth. "Here now, ol pal."

Wouldn't you know, old Ephriam-Ephriam and Billy craned their necks when that there oxen drunk up the mix and smacked its lips like she was good old lappins!

But nothin further noticeable happent.

Which seemed to make the young feller feel a sight better towards everything. "Whew!" says he, puttin the bottle to his mouth.

"Ever drap down now," warns Billy.

And sir, down hit went; down that scrawny skinny throat. And when she was all gone and nothin remained, feller give a belch that like to shook the walls and set down, rubbin at his eyes.

Nobody said nary a word. Hit was as if they was all waitin for Roming candles ta spew forth.

Which didn't happen.

Nothin happent.

"Well," says Billy, gatherin up his hat and lookin pained-pained-pained and disappointy, "give her overnight anyhow. Can't expect miracles."

And that was the old rub: If he had been tellin the truth, and the Devil had told no lie, then they shouldn't a been lookin for nothin else *except* miracles.

Young boy got sad agin and waved farewell as they was about ta leave.

"Thank you kindly anyhow, for—" he begun ta say, when:

"Theee Greee*aaattt*!! O Goddy. Goddy, *Goddy*!" and a bellerin and a hollerin was old Ephriam-Ephriam, his mouth movin ever which way and his eyes rollin around in his head like two eggs.

Great Uncle Billy looked and leapt twenty foot straight up inta the air. "Tom thunder!" he yelled.

And that crippled boy did him some movin too!

Because that old ox, he begun ta moan like a banshee—mooooo*ah*!—and turn blue. *Blue* is what I said: hit went the prettiest shade a sky blue you ever seen, right there in front a the eyes a three witnesses.

"*Babe!*" cries the young feller. "What in *the* world is a happenin?"

Then she rip.

That ox begun to fill out, just exactly like a balloon blowed up with air. The skin begun ta stretch and the old ox ta grow, and whilst she growed she bellered out the lamentations a Job, wheelin and careenin around that there house, mooin and chasin and totally destroyin the furniture.

But all the time growin bigger and bigger and *bigger*. Finally the poor dumb beast let out a whoop and lit for the door, but by the time she got there hit was too small, so she went right on through, takin a whole side a the house with her!

"Oohhh my," moans Ephriam-Ephriam; but when he saw what was beginnin to happen *now*, that poor tired-out old colored gentleman just buckled up and slunk ta the floor in a dead faint.

Do you know what? The young feller, the Stranger, that boy was changin now—right there in the room. *Trans*-formin!

First, his hump melted down to nothin, and that permitted him ta straighten up to his full heighth, which was nice indeed, thank you. Then his twisty legs come whole, and his girth spread —just like with the ox, who was by now half agin as tall as Queen Elizabeth III, who was whinneyin like a thing gone demented.

Now Billy wasn't skeert no more. He looked mostly *inter-ested*, watchin whilst that boy filled out and changed and got bigger and looked no more like a cripple nor I do.

Then he seen the tears a brimmin on the lad's face; so, since he allers did get ashamed and take a aversion when anybody looked like they was goin to thank him or somethin, he picked up Ephriam-Ephriam and lugged him on back to the wagon and clumb in.

The warm breeze was blowin leafs and things over the ground. "Well done," says Billy, his heart fair fit ta bust, "Well done, Satan."

Give a flick with the whip and they jumped ahead, cause Queen Elizabeth III, she was ony too glad ta get out a there.

Took one last look, Billy did; and seen a sight that brung the salt water a rushin. Seen a big strong lad, bigger nor any he had ever seen before, and that ox standin next, both a runnin after the wagon full clip.

"*Heeee*—Giddap!" says Billy, givin her another whup and Queen Elizabeth III took hit at a gallop all the way through the woods, mile after mile.

And Billy settin on the board, cryin, laughin, drinkin his corn soakins, singin till hit woke Ephriam-Ephriam up and all the hooty owls ta boot.

"How come that ox turn blue?" says Ephriam-Ephriam.

"Don't rightly know," says Billy. "How come the boy *not* to?"

"Huh?"

"Somethin in the ox system different from ours, I reckon."

"Huh? Huh?"

Finally hit come pitch black and rain commenced and Billy stopped the wagon.

"Eph," says he, "you know better'n me how ta take care a yourself, the wagon, the business and ekcetera. Am I right?"

The old man looked wondrous and nodded his head.

Billy took his hand and give her a hard old press, then he

kissed Ephriam-Ephriam right smack on the forehead; and havin done so, begun to walk.

Walked a ways and, sure enough, there was Lucifer, the Dark Prince, Mister Devil hisself, settin on a stump, smokin that big old black cigar.

"Wellsir, your honor," says Billy, drunk as drunk, but *good* drunk this time, "I trust you're over your cold."

"Bah!" quoth the Devil, spittin a glob that sizzled the earth where hit fell.

"Heigh-O, well—I'm all ready ta live up ta my part a the bargain, seein as how you did so fine by me."

"BAH!" quoth Satan agin, glarin holes through Billy. "I *oughrt* to take you along just for bein so smarty."

Says Billy: "Don't be rude now. What are you pratin about?"

"About how it's all gone wrong. Wrong, hear? I can't take you."

"Wait a minute, hold on here. When I give *my* word you can be blamed sure hit's the gospel truth! A course you can take me. I'm ready. Let's us go."

"FAUGH!" says Satan. "You was supposed ta use that there wish for *yourself*, like I studied you was goin ta do. Ain't you got brains enough ta know that? Now hit's all ruint. How could you expect me ta take a body's soul cause he done good for somebody *else*?"

Billy thunk her over, then he shook his head sorrowfully. "I don't exactly know what ta say," says he. "Just never considered it, I guess."

Satan drawed up, glowin red hot, madder nor a hornet. "Well, listen here ta me, William Jacob Spiker: Don't you come a toadyin around to me ever agin, hear? Hit's been a humiliatin experience and a total waste a time."

"Well now, I'm sorry. I really am. Isn't they nothin we could fanagle and sort a cheat to—"

"Ohh, go to heaven!" shrieks Satan; and then he sunk through the earth, throwin out sparks and fumes that would a fired the trees if hit wasn't rainin at the time.

Hey ho. Billy. Billy Spiker!

He got ta nigglin and fallin all over hisself gettin back to the wagon.

And he lied a blue streak from then on without nary a qualm until age ninety-four when he passed on as a result of a holt got on him by a Ute injun durin a wrasslin contest.

Yes sir, he were a caution, and that there's his story.

What happent ta who?

What young feller?

Oh—you mean *that* young feller. Let me see now—give me a minute ta study. Blame it, what *was* his name?

Bunyan. Yes sir, that was it: old Paul—I believe that was his first name. Paul Bunyan.

Hear tell he entered the lumber business and took his ox—that blue ox name of Babe—everywhere he went.

Which is plumb fantastical. Now whoever heard of a growed-up man takin a old ox to work and all?

Law!

Body has got to be careful anymore what they accept as solemn fact. They is so many folks without no respect for the truth walkin around, breathin the air.

A Long Way from Capri

"Is in here good enough?" the man asked, pausing at the leather-quilted door.

"I guess so," the girl said. "If it isn't crowded. If it's crowded, let's go somewhere else."

"Whatever you say."

They went into the bar. It was cool and dark and silent. A few couples sat whispering. In a far corner, a piano tinkled aimlessly.

"This is all right," the girl said.

A woman in a formal black dress walked up, holding menus. "Good evening," she murmured, in that soft voice demanded by churches, libraries, cemeteries and good bars. "Cocktails or dinner?"

"Cocktails, I think," the man said.

"This way, please." The hostess turned and walked past the bar. In the half-glow, her dress became transparent from the waist down; it revealed black tights and thin lace stockings.

"If you weren't so serious," the man said, "I'd whistle."

"Go ahead."

The hostess pulled out a table, took their order—two Gibsons—and melted into the darkness, returning moments later, melting away again.

"Now," said the man, who had the sort of gray hair that adds to the look of youth, tan skin, a wrist identification bracelet, and an air of well being, "what's it all about?"

The girl—one thought of her like that, although she was not so much younger than her companion—shook her head. "No," she said, "it's nothing."

"If it's nothing why did you make such a deal out of it? You're here to talk. I'm here to listen."

"I don't want to wreck your evening, Pete."

"You'll wreck it if you don't."

"All right." The girl took a long sip of her Gibson. In the soft light she looked strong and self-sufficient, except for her eyes. "I—"

"Never mind the blindfold. Fire at will."

"Pete, I can't marry you."

The words came out staccato; harsh; final. The man's half-smile vanished. He set his drink down carefully and said, "Come again."

"That's it, that's all; I'm sorry! Now do you see why I—Pete, there isn't any more to say. I can't marry you."

"You mean you want to put it off a while?"

"No!" The girl's fingers clenched. "I mean it's all over. Finished. We're through, Pete."

"Any particular reason?"

"Yes," the girl said. "I—don't love you."

"That's a lie."

"All right; I do love you. But it doesn't make any difference."

"Oh."

"Pete—" She began to pick tiny fragments out of the paper napkin with her fingernails. "We've known each other a little over a year now, haven't we?"

"Year and a half."

"You suppose you know me pretty well?"

"Yeah, that's what I suppose," the man said.

"Tell me about it."

"You're Jeannie Gitmed, thirty-eight, pretty, unattached. Live with your mother. Like sauerkraut. Love a certain engineer. Going to marry that engineer."

The girl's laugh interrupted him. She lit a cigarette and said, "It worked," almost to herself. "They all planned it this way, only for me it worked. And now I've got to ruin it."

"You're not coming through."

She ran a hand through her hair. "Okay," she said, "get ready." The napkin dropped, shredded. "During the war," she said, "I was a field worker. I was sent to Italy early in 1944 and I stayed there till 1946. When I joined I was broke; a couple of years later I came out with thirty-five thousand dollars."

The man said nothing for a moment; then, "Go on."

"You really want me to?"

"Yes."

"At Capri," the girl said, "there were a few women and a lot of soldiers. A lot of sick, lonely, frightened guys. They'd been on a lot of missions and they knew that in a week or so they'd have to go out on more missions and fly some more and maybe get killed. They were scared, and hungry. They needed—" She sighed and shook her head again. "No; if I'm going to tell it, I might as well tell it straight, the way it was. The truth is, I wasn't thinking of the poor boys at all. It might have started out that way—I guess it did; I can't remember—but it turned into something else. I think I was just like a hundred other girls: I saw a good thing and I grabbed at it. Nothing else. I was young and bored. And tired of living like a churchmouse. So I started saying yes to the fellows, and I started accepting their gifts. Fifty dollar gifts, never less, sometimes more." She stared at the man with the short gray hair.

He said nothing.

"Do you understand what I'm saying, Pete? I was a whore. A prostitute. It was a perfect opportunity—away from home, in a strange place where no one knew me. And the servicemen all had pockets full of money—money they couldn't spend because there was no place to spend it. Capri wasn't quite the paradise then that it's supposed to be now. They could work the black market, and they could swing deals—but what good did it do, when they knew they might not live till next week? So they —well, they never resented the fact that I was getting rich. It didn't matter. Besides—" her voice became hard and steady "—I always gave them their money's worth."

Still the gray-haired man did not speak.

"I was pretty," the girl said, harshly, "and young, and American. But I still had to work, because the boys wanted more than just a roll in the hay for their fifty bucks. They wanted love and passion and warmth and sincerity and everything. They wanted an affair. So I obliged. After a while it got to be easy: I just closed my eyes, put on an act, and it went over. It went over with lieutenants and privates and corporals and captains—and even a general, once. They all thought I was mad about them; them alone. Which shows I must have been pretty good at the job, because I almost never even saw what they looked like. Besides, there were so many . . ."

The man sat rigidly, never moving his eyes from the girl's face.

"Not much point in going on with it," she said.

"I'd like you to."

She looked at the tabletop. "That's about it. But if you're waiting for a chance to be noble—I know all about the Allison family's sense of pride—the Allisons of Boston!—well, forget it. I don't have any excuses. I regret it, now, of course, Lord yes —but they all regret it some time. Then, I didn't care much one way or the other, and I went on not caring for a long time. Up until recently, as a matter of fact. When I met you. But—I didn't hate it or enjoy it or look on it as anything but an easy way to make a quick killing. The risk was small, the hours were short, and I ended up with enough to last six or seven years."

She tapped another cigarette loose. "And that's the whole story. I can almost see your parents falling over with heart attacks! They—what'd you say?—they think I'm such a nice level-headed girl. 'A credit to our son in his social position!' I *could* ease the blow by slipping in a starving old mother or a sister I wanted to put through college, or something—most of them had lines like that—but it just doesn't happen to be true. Mom and I were poor, all right, but not that poor. Not by a long shot." She nervously stubbed the cigarette out and continued to stare at the table. "The ending is short. After the war and six months of traveling, I went back home. I cooked up a fancy lie for my mother —something about combat pay, extra duty, that kind of thing —and moved here. We've managed to get along ever since."

"Is that all?"

"Just about. When I met you, I realized, I think I saw that never knowing anyone before like Peter Allison was maybe one of the reasons I did it in the first place. I'd never been in love, or close to it. But so what?" Her voice lowered. "I've never let a man touch me since then, either; but again, so what? What does it mean? Look, Pete, I'm no good. Right up to tonight I was actually planning to marry you and never say a word about it. Become one of the social set: Mrs. Allison!"

"And what stopped you?" the man asked.

"Fear, mostly. Maybe we could have been a happily married couple, just like in the movies. But maybe—well, I see a real beautiful picture. I see us wheeling the babies to church one fine morning a couple of years from now. It's a nice day and you've just been made vice-president or something, because you're such a nice fellow and you have such a fine respectable family. We pass a man going in the opposite direction, a stranger. We don't even notice him. But he notices us. He turns around and runs back. And he says, 'Hey, I'll be doggoned if it isn't little Jeannie, the sweetheart of the troops! Remember me, Jeannie, Lieutenant Joe Smith? Remember?'" She shuddered visibly. "Anyway, you'd find out eventually. I had an awful lot of customers. One of them would be bound to show up. Any questions?"

"No," the man said.

"Then let's get out of here." The girl touched the man's hand. "I'm sorry, Pete. It was great while it lasted. I'm—sorry."

"About telling me?"

"No, about everything."

Suddenly the man smiled. "You love me, Jeannie," he said.

"Sure, yes; but so what? What difference could that make? I know you come from a family of 'gentlemen' but the noble act won't work. You'd spend the rest of your life kicking yourself."

The man threw back his head and laughed, loudly. Then, abruptly, he stopped. "Jeannie, you're so very sure of yourself, of the world," he said. "And so sure you're going to have to pay for those years . . ."

"Stop it, Pete."

He took her hands and held them tightly. "Not 'Pete,'" he said. "The name's Smith. Lieutenant Joe Smith. Remember?"

The girl's eyes widened.

He laughed again. "I'm sorry, honey, but it's true. We're both a long way from Capri, but I never forgot. You see, you were so busy worrying about *your* past that you never tried to find out anything about mine. In 1944 I was flying a B-24 in the 15th Air Force. They gave me a week on the island. I was—how'd you say?—sick, lonely and frightened. Somebody told me about a girl who was very nice. I had a bucket of flight pay and nowhere to spend it . . ."

The girl tried to speak.

"When you came into the office that time," the man went on, "I recognized you—right away. I remembered. And that's one of the reasons I asked Fred to introduce us."

"You're lying!"

"Nope. I have proof. Incidentally, you're right: you did do a good job."

"Pete—"

"Now, I figure we ought to have a real simple ceremony. Just a few friends. Then a week in Mexico, and—"

The woman in the transparent gown appeared out of the darkness. "Is everything all right?" she asked, sweetly.

The man smiled. "I think so," he said. "I think you could say that everything's all right."

With the Family

He waited until all the ice cubes had melted, then he said, "Solly, an exact replica."

The bartender, who was Irish but did not resemble a Toby mug, turned from his television set reluctantly. He blinked.

"On-the-rocks, Mr. Gallagher?"

"Exactly, if you mean my order. But if you mean my life, well, you're not far off there either. On-the-rocks, Solly."

Gallagher glanced about the bar, which was deserted with the exception of an unattractive red-head who had fallen asleep. He picked up his wet cigarette and stared at it for a while but, for some reason, that made him feel ill, so instead he watched the bartender's expert movements with a glass, three round ice cubes and some scotch, unspecified—Gallagher couldn't tell the difference.

"Solly," he said, "do I look like a first class rat to you? If you'll promise to tell the truth I'll pay for the next five drinks in advance."

The bartender looked at Gallagher, shrugged, decided not to smile and switched off the TV, which featured at the time a wrestling match.

"No sir, you sure don't."

"Now look, I'll do the patronizing in this place. Out with it: Do I, or do I not, look to you like a first class rat?"

The bartender sighed and pulled over a stool and sat down.

"Okay; on second thought you do, at that."

"Ah *ha*! Well, I'm not. That's what she's thinking right now at this very minute, but I'm not. The conclusion is crude and obvious. I'll tell you a little story, Solly, if your heart is sound and your stomach isn't weak. Would you like to hear a story, Solly, true-to-life and full of pathos?"

"Nothing I'd like more," the bartender said, sighing so hard it created a rumble in his throat. "Just a minute." He slid open the glass door behind the bar and took from the second shelf a bottle, unmarked: some of the contents of this he poured into a glass, adding water but no ice.

"All set? A plaintive lament from your infinitely sad strings, Bela. The lights: Turn them down. Now then. Solly, they say if you scratch a bartender you'll find a cynic. You a cynic?"

"No."

"Excellent. A cynical person might not appreciate the irony of my little fable. But you want facts, not frippery. Right?"

"Right."

"Right. Okay. What I'm driving at is this—it would have been different if it was any other Christmas. Any other, you think I'd give a hoot? Not on your life. But this was our first god-damn Christmas, very first! Isn't there anything sacred in a first Christmas together anymore? Is there to *you*, Solly?"

"Every time, Mr. Gallagher."

"Bet your boots, Dad. I'm a fair person, I can see three or four sides to any damn question. On the other hand, I'm firm, know what I mean? *Firm*—not obstinate. Know what the first thing she said was? Told me about that promise I made. Who wouldn't have? Here we're only married six lousy months: she asks me would I mind spending Christmas with her folks. Said she'd never spent one away from them and they'd be hurt to tears and would I itsy-bitsy mind. For God's sakes, what was I going to do—start a big brawl on that little point? Not that I liked the idea, but I figured I'd talk her out of it when the time came, you know? *Sure* I said yes. All right, I *promised*, if you want to put it that way. What the hell else could I do?"

"You done what any man would, Mr. Gallagher. You're posi-tively right."

"Don't be condescending—at least until you've heard the whole story. But first, a restoration job on your masterpiece, this time *con amore*."

The red-head looked up in astonishment, opened her eyes very wide, and went back to sleep. She wore a good leather jacket inscribed FLYIN' LIONS—Oaklawn, Illinois, and a cotton cap which was fastened to her hair with a hairpin.

Gallagher took out a cigarette and patted his pockets for his lighter, which wasn't in any of them, and tried to get the cigarette back into the pack. It wouldn't go in easily so he said "Damn" and took a light from the bartender.

"A toast, Solly," he said, "to all the stupid women in the world who are just plain stupid, and to all the intelligent ones . . . ditto. And a flagon of llama dung on the in-betweens."

The bartender folded his towel over the rack and sipped his drink.

A man and a woman, both dressed formally, came into the bar, looked around and went out again, without speaking.

"So I said yes. I would have signed a writ if she'd asked me to then, but like she says, so sweetly: 'I trusted your word, Jack.' Our first Christmas; first in the world: tonight. This very merry Yuletide night, Solly! Even you haven't wished me so much as a joyous Noel yet, you know that, don't you?"

"Yes I did, Mr. Gallagher. First thing I said when you came in. I said 'Merry Christmas.' But you didn't answer."

Gallagher gasped, affectedly. "What? Unforgiveable! Now you'll *never* believe I'm not a first class rat."

"Go on with your story. What happened then?"

"Well, she didn't mention it until tonight is why I got so sore, I guess. What a thing to spring on me! Hell, man, I'd forgotten all about six months ago and whatever I said then. Know what? I'd planned a surprise: Here's what it was. I was going to take her out to Ciro's first for just a few quick ones, then a crinkly Christmas drive out toward the beach. Malibu, Paradise Cove . . . That has a special meaning you'll be gentleman enough not to ask me about, I hope. But after the drive, we'd go home to our apartment, see, and I had Sam plant the big present, the Saks gown and that beautiful rust-colored overcoat from Bullocks. She didn't know about these. We'd come back—there'd be the tree, all lit up, and all the presents and a bottle of champagne—Krug, too, damn it, '27, like in Bemelmans—and we'd open up the presents, hers last, and then—Oh nuts, Solly, it would have been a ball. Perfect. Anne's not stupid, for God's sakes—I'd never marry a stupid woman again, not after Nell. Remember Nell, Solly?"

"Never had the pleasure, Mr. Gallagher."

"Neither did I. My first wife. A real dog, believe me, in spades. Anne's different, though: Class, beauty, all that—but a human being, know that I mean, Solly? A real honest-to-God human being? Why, she's so human she admitted once she didn't hate Hollywood. That takes guts."

"A lot to be said for a girl'd say that."

"Yeah; especially her coming from New York. Know what she said about New York? Listen to this: 'A dresser drawer full of big white worms couldn't be more stifling, unhealthy or repugnant.' How's that?"

"Mr. Gallagher," the bartender said solemnly, "I'd say you've got a pretty fine girl for a wife." He smiled at Gallagher, who smiled back, and they drank considerably, both of them. Then Gallagher frowned.

"One hell of a way to spend Christmas, ain't it though? I mean, truthfully speaking for a minute."

"From your point of view I'd say it sure is. 'Course, I have mine tomorrow when we're closed, and you get used to that. What was it, kid—get in a fight with your wife? Because if you did you ought to go and make up. You'll be sorry. C'mon, little lady's probably crying her eyes out right this second."

"My ass," Gallagher said, and asked for another drink. "Huh-uh," he said when he got the drink, "the little lady is at this precise second whooping it up with the most hideous assortment of relatives you could dig up if you tried. Cool bunch of people: How they ever had Anne beats the hell out of me. Take the old man, for instance. Pompous old poop, worth a steady twenty-two five every damn year of the world; high mucky-muck with some traffic agency here. They transferred him to head their L.A. branch: that's why Anne came. Big man! Wears a moustache that he dyes black and looks like a con man who happened to inherit some loot. And the mother—oh my God. God save us, Solly. I thought her species went out with the duck-billed platypus. Doesn't like me. Know why? She doesn't exactly think she exactly approves of the advertising business. 'They're so unstable, I hear.' Old bat has a good fifty of her own—but think either one of 'em would help me out a nickel's worth? When I could have parlayed a stinking ten grand stake into a small fortune? Don't worry; I've met some of the aunts and uncles, too. Brrr."

Gallagher shuddered so that the ice cubes rattled in his glass. The bartender looked confused and sympathetic.

"A motley crew, Solly. Motliest in the world. Gang of starched shirts and bleached girdles and square cats, believe me. And they're all there, Solly, every last one of 'em. What's this? Do I detect disbelief in your saturnine features? Marvelous. I knew I came to the right place. Yes, my dearest friend, that is what my wife, Anne, proposed. That is what my wife, Anne, asked—nay, *demanded*—at five-thirty this afternoon. Today. After my surprise was planned and everything . . ."

"Don't seem right. What'd you do, finally?"

"I hit her in the mouth with a steam iron and then kicked at her prostrate form, of course. Or should have. No; what I did was make an utter ass out of myself. I said no, she said yes, I said absolutely no, she said positively—now, we'd never even quarrelled before this, you understand. Not a peep: the picture of impeccably perfect domesticity. And every other weekend we'd trot over to Westwood and 'look in' on Mr. and Mrs. Henderson, too. Never, as I say, Solly, a peep from me about this. It was hell, but I never complained."

"That must have gave her ideas. Women for you."

"Yeah. You suppose? No. That's not Anne: she's too shrewd. That's why she didn't mention Christmas until today, either—oh, I'm telling you, the woman's smart. Thought she'd catch me with my pants down, I'd remember my promise even without her reminding me, and we'd spend a glorious beautiful first Christmas with the family. With the family—oi weh!"

"So what'd you do after the fight?"

"Said a few words into the microphone, grinned at the screaming throng and modestly made my way back to the dressing room. That is, here, Solly."

The bartender shook his head. "I get it now, Mr. Gallagher. You just skipped out and made the little woman feel terrible and now you're sorry and want to get with it but you don't feel you ought to as a man. Isn't it?" he said.

Gallagher looked up from his drink. His face contained a number of expressions, none of them cheerful.

"Solly! They told me barkeeps were all philosophers; but I didn't know your breed was psychic too! With what simplicity you reduce my problem: like a combination Spinoza, Dunninger, and Eleanor Roosevelt. One correction, however: I'm not so sure I'm sorry. If I am, I've got a hunch it's for myself. Aren't you at all sorry for me?"

"Sure, sure. But—you know what you got to do in the end anyway, don't you?"

Gallagher clutched his glass, leaned over and glared at the bartender, whose face was pitted and laced with a thousand burst blood vessels and so could not look anything but sincere.

"What—what have I got to do?" Gallagher asked, poising the rim of the glass approximately one-sixteenth of an inch from his lower lip.

The bartender permitted the vaguest suggestion of the inscrutable to disorganize his features, shrugged in an expression of inevitability and walked over to wait on a thin man with spectacles who had walked in quietly.

When the thin man had downed his drink, said "Ah" discreetly and left, Gallagher assumed a hangdog look. His ice cubes were wilting again.

"Do I have to?" he said, plaintively.

"What else—sit here all night?"

There was acerbity in Gallagher's voice. "No, by God, if that's your attitude. I'll go elsewhere for my refreshment."

"Now, now, I didn't mean anything wrong. Get loaded to the teeth if that's what you want. You pay your money, I'll fix the booze. I only meant, well, you asked advice."

"I did no such thing. You're too used to lushes and their problems. I was only edifying you with what I took to be a charming story in the modern vein—no beginning, no end: all middle —together with the proper ironical twist. Solly—" Gallagher softened, "—I suppose I'll have to, won't I?"

"Yeah," the bartender said slowly, reaching over and turning his television back on, only without the sound.

"She's still there, you know that."

"Uh-huh."

"And I'll have to face them all, every one, and it'll be god-awful. Lord! Anne will come over and kiss my cheek, damn her, and the old bat'll say, 'John, we're so sorry you were detained. A pity, my boy. You missed the party and the opening of the god-damn presents.' Then what'll I do?"

"It's a tough life sometimes, Mr. Gallagher. Next year you'll forget all about this."

"'Our first Christmas, darling.' Rats. Okay, Solly, here's your ducats. I'm in your debt, Daddy-O. Never would have had the guts to go back without some help." Gallagher stumbled slightly as his foot missed the lower stop to the bar; he felt a rush of dizziness and stood still for a few moments.

"You okay, Mr. Gallagher?"

"Touch of jungle fever, Pops. It'll pass. She's a wonderful girl, Solly, really. Wouldn't ever do this for nobody but Anne; you got to remember that. For Anne: upward, onward, into the lions' den, into the mouth of—Jesus! Well, Merry Christmas, old poop. If I don't come out of it alive you can tell your grand-children you murdered the sweetest guy you ever knew."

The bartender smiled openly. "Good night, Mr. Gallagher. You're doin' what any red-blooded man would do. Merry Christmas!"

Gallagher turned to wave and knocked into a table, upsetting two chromium chairs and a false candle. At the noise the unat-tractive red-headed woman sat bolt-upright and shrieked: "All right, all right, leave me alone for two minutes, will you!" and closed her eyes.

Gallagher went out the door.

Two hours later he came back in the door.

His suit was a bit more wrinkled than it had been; his hand-kerchief dangled from its pocket and his tie was loosened and pulled down. There was no order to his hair. His glasses had slid on his nose. He looked displaced.

The bartender did not seem happy to see him.

"Shut up," he said to the bartender and went back to his stool. Everything was the same in the big room. The woman still sat straight up and her eyes were still shut. There was a 21-inch view of the Santa Claus parade on the TV and the two chairs had been set aright.

"Chickened out, huh? You still got time, you know."

Gallagher was quiet for a while, merely sitting, with his chin cupped in his hands. After a time he said: "On-the-rocks, Petronius. And get out the weeping vase."

"Bad?"

"Oh no, not really. No worse than any run-of-the-mill public hanging." He got a glimpse of his tie in the violet-tinted mirror that never flattered him anyway and started to make adjustments, but the knot wouldn't slide so he gave it up.

"No, Solly," he said, "I didn't lose my nerve. Never was a stouter soldier in the face of doom, s'help me. But it wasn't any use."

"Mean she wasn't there—went out to look for you!"

"About your sense of humor—she was there, all right. With bells on."

"Yeah?"

"Let me paint you a canvas, Solly. It isn't a pretty picture, but you might be impressed. Like Goya? He might have captured some of it; not all, for damn sure. Maybe Dali. Anyway——" here Gallagher disposed of one half of his drink "——I jump in the car all full of Yuletide forgiveness and superhuman understanding, see? I barrel a cool seventy all the way down Sunset and over to their place. I don't think, I don't remember. Not even hurt! I pull in the driveway, next to this Cadillac and that Cadillac—a whole fleet of 'em, Solly. I look like a bum: already it starts. You don't drive a Caddie, do you?"

The bartender shook his head imperiously. "I favor a Dodge, Mr. Gallagher. Good dependable trans—"

"Don't. Well, the place you'd think would be blazing with lights, but she's darker than a tomb when I got out. Across the street I could hear 'God Rest Ye Merry Gentlemen,' and I swear to you it sounded like a dirge! Now get this: I was going to dash in with my usual devil-may-care likeable grin that's so winning, chuck the old lady under the chin, tell 'em a tall tale and scoop Anne up. Fair, Solly? More than fair, considering I'd rather have been in Mouse Breath, Idaho."

Horns had begun to honk along the boulevard outside, and the sounds filtered through the padded leather doors. Gallagher's head ached.

"I was going to apologize, even."

"Don't feel bad about it. I've apologized to my wife once in a while. You get over it afterwards."

"Wait, now, you haven't come to the good part yet. I knocked nimbly on the door, without hesitation, mind you, and I think I whistled a carol while I waited. Then the door creaks slowly open and there's this woman all dressed in black with a pale face, glaring at me. Who is it?"

"The housekeeper?"

"Good try. No; it's Mrs. Henderson. She looks me up, she looks me down, and I thought for a minute she was going to vomit. 'Merry Christmas, John' she said. Then Milly steps up and takes my coat and silently I follow Mrs. Henderson down the dark hall to the living room. And there—oh God, give me another drink, will you."

Gallagher had little color left in his face, and his hands trembled. The bartender poured a light one.

"There they all are, Solly, every one of them, sitting there in that room. Uncle Fred, Aunt Billie, the Johnstons, this uncle, that: the place is crawling with them. And there in the center, on the big throne, is the old man in his soup & fish, looking just like somebody had given him the job of dissecting a cockroach."

"What about your wife?"

"Magnificent! She's sitting on the arm of that chair with a mildewed handkerchief in her fist, eyes red, jaw slack, expression accusatory and bewildered and hurt more than you could ever know. You get the tableau, Solly?"

"Dirty rotten shame, Mr. Gallagher. Must have been rough."

"I'd rather be on the first wave at Iwo any day. But remember, no one's saying a bloody word. All just sitting around, with only the Christmas tree lights on, just sitting and staring at me."

"What did you say to them?"

"I said, 'Anyone for tennis?' but it didn't go over so good. Anne too, the worst of them; especially when she heaves that sob and turns her face. Weh! The old man coughs and says: 'Too bad you got tied up, Jack, you missed a fine time. Oh well, couldn't be helped I suppose?' He knew damn well where I had been, even if Anne *had* cooked one up. Even I could smell me. But that's what the slimy old poop said. Thank God he didn't smile!"

"I wonder what I would have done . . ."

"You'd have wished them a Merry Christmas. Right?"

"I don't know."

"Well, that's what I did. I said 'Merry Christmas, everybody' —and then, one by one, the crows got up and walked over and planted a kiss on my cheek. Yeah! The kiss of death, Solly—I shook in my boots, all the time trying to shoot a glance Anne's way. Think she'd see me? Hell no. Then I make the rounds of the boys, pumping *their* fishy hands. So far, so ghastly."

The bartender didn't seem to notice the fat man who had taken a seat over in a dark corner. The fat man drummed his fingers a while, walked up to the far side of the bar and then went away.

Gallagher tapped his glass on the counter nervously. "Still not the worst, though. We come now to the *pièce de résistance*. After the unholy ritual, where nobody said anything but mumble, I put on a grin and went over to the punch bowl and got some goo. I got back, the waxworks was still in session. I looked forward to a beautiful evening. Then—the meat-axe right between my eyes."

"What happened?"

"Fragile, delicate Mrs. Henderson waddled over, looked me right in the teeth and made a gesture with her finger over to the tree. There were all the presents, Solly, all unwrapped and out and the wrapping piled neatly to one side. All, that is, except mine. Mine they'd left, and they were stacked at the foot of the tree, gaily bedecked in ribbons red and green."

The bartender shuddered visibly. "Oh no, Mr. Gallagher!"

"Oh *yes!*" So I opened each present, one by one, Solly: a pipe from Cousin Albert, a dressing gown from Auntie Cora, a leather traveling kit from whoozis. I smile, I say 'Wonderful' and the word echoes in the silence. I go over and peck Aunt Lucy and shake hands with Uncle Fred, and I open another present and another one and—forever and ever!

"Last, of course, they fork over a big package and I open it. From Anne—mine to her were still home, see. A sport coat I'd had my eye on for months but couldn't ever afford. Anne's blubbering by this time, naturally, and dabbing at her eyes quietly. 'Thanks, darling.' I didn't try to kiss her. Hit me again."

The bartender did not go light on this one. He went very heavy.

"Hope I've not bored you. There's only one more part, and that's it, but it's quite a refinement. While I'm standing there with the sport coat hanging from my arm, looking stupid and feeling like a sex murderer in front of an all woman jury, *then* I get it. Anne leaps up out of the stillness, looks at me a minute and says, 'Oh, Jack, why did you have to spoil everything?' Up to her room or someplace, like a shot. The old man shifts in his chair and tells me: 'Pity, Jack my boy. Anne had a surprise all planned out. She was going to drive you to Malibu or some-such right after our little party. Too bad.'"

In putting his head on his arms, Gallagher hit his glass which overturned.

"Tune in tomorrow, folks, for the next episode of John's Second Wife," he said thickly.

The bartender said nothing. He looked embarrassed, somehow, and he turned his TV on again.

Then Gallagher's head snapped up and pivoted towards the corner. He looked as if he'd suddenly remembered an appointment. "Solly," he said, "would you please tell me why you haven't done anything about that young lady over there?" He pointed in the direction of the red-headed woman, who did not stir.

"Her? I asked her hours ago if she was with anybody, but she said no, to leave her alone. Cold sober then, so—live and let live tonight, I say."

"Well, but, hold on, man—poor dear girl must be lonely. Wait! Two birds with one stone. I'll share my unhappiness with a kindred spirit."

Gallagher winked, then began to walk unsteadily to the woman's table. He sat down and said some things to her, but the woman kept saying "Go away, will you, will you please" so after a while he got up and took some bills from his wallet. He gave the bills to the bartender.

"Merry Christmas," he said.

"Same to you, Mr. Gallagher. Don't worry, it'll all work out okay, you'll see."

"Yeah."

Gallagher smiled and made his way to the door, went back for his glasses but he had put them in his pocket so he smiled again at the bartender and walked outside.

There wasn't anyone waiting for him.

Moon in Gemini

Charles Beaumont and J.E. Tomerlin

Outside, the street was filled with light; bright hot midsummer sunlight, and it made Jodi dizzy. It caused her eyes to pinch together, smarting. But this was not the first time she had been made dizzy going from the tomb coolness of Penn station to the city's afternoon glare, so she blinked a few times and pushed on through the big glass door.

There were many people downtown on the streets. A shining river of people, all hurrying, all bound for destinations. Faceless big-city people, baked lobster red in the sun or turned the color of wet paste. Jodi felt herself caught up, like a leaf tossed into a fast current, and soon she was hurrying along with the people.

But no one looked at her, as she expected they might; and this was, at first, a little disappointing. There were no rude stares: for that matter, no motherly smiles either. It wasn't any different at all. They just hurried along.

And Jodi thought, *They don't know, any of them. Know or care or even think about it. They have no idea—why, they've got a mother in their midst!*

The phrase reminded her of Jim, and as she walked fast she thought of just how he might say it: "A mothah in theiuh mid-sst!" And how he'd break into a grin afterwards, much more like a college sophomore than a dignified office manager.

Her eyes adjusted to the bright city dazzle, and now the warmth that passed through her clothes and touched her skin felt good. She walked a full block before realizing it was in exactly the opposite direction she had wished to go.

She broke from the clot of hurrying people, and started back. For no particular reason, though: there was over an hour to kill. An hour before she would meet Jim at Child's for lunch; and then, the ride back home on the train. Hours and hours, almost the whole day away from Mother Hilton.

That made her feel even better. It was the first afternoon she'd had alone with Mark, actually the first! It would, of course, be Mark; it couldn't be anything but a boy. She knew. Certain exceptionally intuitive women know these things, that's all. Mother Hilton could rave on as much as she wanted to about the chances of its being a girl. As much as she wanted to: she was wrong, wrong, in spite of her years of experience.

Jim, I'll tell you the truth. I came to have lunch with you because your mother is driving me crazy. Now don't look so alarmed. I hate her. But no more than she hates me. What? You thought we were getting on so wonderfully? Well, that's how much you know. Your darling mother would hate anybody you married—that's what she doesn't realize. Listen to me. It's very simple. She's always had you, you see, and now she doesn't want to lose you. You marry somebody, she loses you. Of course it's foolish, but that's the way mothers are, that's their nature. All mothers are insane. Or at least they get that way. Want to know something else? I could have taken the 10:20 and got here right on time. But if I'd been left alone another hour— just one more hour—with Mother, *I would have gone quietly, calmly crazy.* That's *how wonderfully we're getting on, my darling husband!*

Jodi stopped in a doorway so she could taste the words. She wished she could record them and take the recording home and play it to herself every night. She thought briefly of going to some company and getting it done. But the thought passed. It was childish. Besides, Jim might get hold of it. . .

She looked into the window of a surgical supply store, and the wavery ghost of a woman looked back. A woman with a rather attractive face—certainly not bad, anyway—framed in shoulder-length hair the color of roasted chestnuts. Fine wide eyes, a little puzzled always, and a full mouth pulled up at the corners now, as if in amusement.

Pretty good for six months along, Jodi thought and grinned. Then she saw the man inside looking at her. She glanced down at her stomach and a warm red came to her cheeks, because the man was actually staring, or half-staring. Not rudely. So she turned and reentered the bright flow of people.

She wants to eat us up, Jim. Really. Believe me. She says she's just visiting, but you watch! That visit will last a long time. First it's to take care of me until Mark's born. Next it'll be to do what she can to take the burden off my shoulders once the baby is here. And after that, she'll think of something. Oh, they're clever! She'll wait till Mark is healthy, then she'll set about driving us apart so she can have not only you but our little boy too! Just look at the row we had last night—don't you really know who caused it? Don't you?

Poor Jim. He'd just stand there pop-eyed, with that agonized, hurt, utterly bewildered look plastered all over his face. "Jodi!" he'd say, like Moses or somebody. "*Jo*-di!"

Grown men shouldn't have mothers, Jodi thought. She remembered the black satin woman who'd sat next to her on the train. A miserable creature, unquestionably a mother. She'd so wanted to be alone, to think; naturally it was her luck to sit next to a phrenologist, or whatever it was palm-readers called themselves. Such a delightful woman. The way she'd taken Jodi's hand and studied it, like a map . . .

You're by nature very quiet and reserved, aren't you honey? Sensitive, easily hurt. But you keep your little hurts to yourself. Oh yes, and you treasure your own personal thoughts. Sometimes that's very good, because it can give you a lot of secret satisfaction; but it can be bad, too, because you're more likely to let little differences grow into important problems. Oh yes, and you fear physical pain.

And how she'd then taken Jodi's right hand, and said darkly:

Your right hand shows what's actually going to happen to you—your future life and all. Now, here's your love-line, see? Well, well. I see you've had two loves.

Now how in the world had the old harridan guessed that?

The first: fiery, wonderful, but it cooled. The second, more stable, quieter. You will love him very much. But—something will happen. Yes, I see a tragedy, a loss. A black loss.

Crazy woman, didn't she have any sense? Even though Jodi *hadn't* experienced any of the sensations you're supposed to when you're pregnant, even so, it might have seriously upset her. Crazy woman. Going around frightening people with her cheap bridge-party magic . . .

She was in a cluster of people now, at a curb, waiting for the light to change. She shook the memory of the woman on the train, Mother Hilton, swept it all from her mind and concentrated on being a young girl in a big city. But there was a voice, strident and harsh, twangy with dialect, coming from the mid-twenties fur-piece in front of her:

"—not another one, really! Oh, I mean, how awful. I mean, after losing two already!"

And from the second wide back, the second waiting woman:

"Well, you know Margaret. Rolls right off her. I give my pity to poor Mr. Scott."

"You mark my words: She'll keep this up and kill herself as well as all them babies."

"Swear, you'd think folks'd learn, wouldn't you? I mean, after all, I mean there's *some* women that just weren't meant to have children."

Shut up, Jodi thought. *Please shut up. I'm not sick, I'm not crazy, I'm perfectly healthy and my baby will be perfectly healthy, and I refuse to listen to you. There's always people like you, trying to make it hard, trying to scare us, make it as miserable as it possibly can be.*

"A'course, the first 'un is always the hardest. Lordy! I like to just about died with my Billy, it was so bad."

That's right. Keep it up, you witches. Tell us about how your children were all Mongoloid idiots. They probably were; I hope so, anyway. No I don't. Oh—light, please change, please change . . .

The two women with the coarse voices did not seem to see Jodi, and they chattered along as their feet carried them with a rush across the street.

Jodi lingered at the curb, feeling the small panic touch her. She thought about a lot of things, now, but all unclearly: the row with Jim last night, Mother Hilton and her only-married-once-and-to-a-fine-old-family eyes that seemed to say, "Really, child, are you asking us to believe that *you* are going to be a mother and take up a mother's responsibilities?" She thought of Jim's eyes, big, amber, and how they'd widened full of great wonder when she'd told him.

Well, it's about time I started feeling dizzy, she laughed to herself, then, and stepped off the curb. A shriek ripped loud and a car bobbled on its chassis a few feet from her. The driver wore a look of exasperation which lasted until he'd taken in Jodi's profile. Then he smiled sheepishly. She jumped back onto the curb and breathed deeply. The light had been red.

Stupid women. Stupid silly women. They'd frightened her with their idiotic talk. "—there's some women that just weren't meant to have children . . ."

Having a baby wasn't such a big thing, was it, for Heaven's sake! Millions of women had them, every day. What was it—two hundred every minute, everywhere in the world?

But how very strange that she hadn't actually thought about it until just now, now at this second, here on the curb of a street she'd crossed ten thousand times . . .

She was going to be a mother!

"Oops lady, I'm awful sorry." A man smiled at her and took off down the canyon full of people again.

Jodi stamped her foot so no one could see. What in the world was this that had hold of her? It was normal, wasn't it? All right, if you're not a child, not a scared little girl, wait for the light and go across the damned street!

The light went to green again. And cars came around to make left turns, and she saw how hard the cars were—steel and metal and hard sharp corners and tons of weight—and she thought of how soft, how very soft that large and gentle rise in her stomach was . . .

The brakes shrieked again and a terrible picture exploded in her mind.

So she turned and didn't cross the street. No need to anyway, really: she was just walking, just killing time.

The department store loomed big and green and cool in the hot afternoon and, fighting down the sudden sick feeling, Jodi went inside. The terror seemed to stay out in the bright sun. She felt good once more, and the thoughts melted in the air-conditioned comfort.

Wonderful. She could pick up that tie Jim had decided not to buy. "Got to conserve now, honey . . ."

Let's see. Ties: Men's Wear: Fourth Floor.

The elevator doors whirred open and the car disgorged its magpie women passengers and meek embarrassed uncomfortable men and Jodi went inside and it filled up again. A click of castanets and the doors whirred closed another time.

The car moved up with a sudden sickening lurch. It was so crowded. Lots of people. Lots of—sharp elbows, carefully avoiding her. How many people? Twelve? That made twenty-four elbows. She was in a car with twenty-four elbows!

It lurched up and someone said: "Second floor. Out, anyone?" and more people got in, though none got out. How many elbows now? Not to mention hundreds of toes. And counting toes and fingers, that came to—

It wasn't any use. She had to think about it. The car was full and it was heavy, and maybe it was *too* heavy. What if the cables that held the car and pulled it so many dizzy feet up the cold damp shaft, what if these slender threads should—break? Even here, on the second floor? What if they should break?

"Third floor. Lingerie, hosiery, baby clothes—"

"Let me out," Jodi heard herself cry. "This is my floor. Let me out, *please*."

The crowd parted with surprising ease, leaving her standing foolish and frightened in front of the elevator with all the people inside looking at her curiously.

Jodi turned and walked away quickly. No use. She'd have to get out of the store and back in the streets. Out of the store, anyway. It was stifling now, full of human sweat and no air, not cool anymore.

She heard the elevator go up and watched the arrow point to the number, Four. Five; Six; Seven; then, down again, stopping, pausing, and she watched until the arrow pointed at One.

Jodi sighed. But, somehow, it didn't make her feel any better. She couldn't go inside that little cage a second time, because —well, she couldn't. She fought the picture of the elevator plummeting down floor after floor like a rock dropped into a clear pool, falling, falling, and crashing on the hard cement below.

"May I help you?"

"No. No, thank you, I was only—"

Of course, there was the escalator. What could be simpler and safer?

But it was like peering into the wrong end of a telescope, and it made her clutch the rail. The rail moved under her fingers, pulling her arm along, trying to throw her off balance. She pulled back and watched.

Alice fell a long way, she thought. *Down, down, down; curiouser and curiouser . . .*

Jodi gave a little cry as someone jostled her and she found her feet on the spined and shiny surface of the moving stairs. The baby! Oh, she thought, she should have left it at home, with Mother Hilton. Why should it terrify her so when she didn't even know its name—not really. *It*—not a boy, not a girl, not even a human being yet. A formless blob of softness that she had with her, something that would probably scare her to death if she'd meet it in a dark alley some night . . . And yet, she shielded that part of her that carried this strange thing, and was quite prepared to fight with her life for its safety.

Why? Why was this so?

The stairs collapsed one into another, like accordion pleats, like a Chinese puzzle; hard sharp stairs this second, flat pieces of steel the next.

They were going to kill her. The thought arrived fully dressed. It was what everyone expected. They'd not wanted her to marry Jim: she a secretary and a divorcee, and he the most eligible—That man behind her. *Of course!* Mother Hilton had hired him. Mother Hilton knew what would happen between him and her if anything happened to the baby—or she thought she knew. So she hired someone to follow her and push her down the stairs.

The stairs collapsed again into themselves, and she found herself on the ground floor. And the man behind her was walking with another woman, walking away, whistling some tune.

Jodi looked around her and everything began to swim before her eyes, as goldfish swim in a bowl when the water has been clouded by their movement. The killers were around her every-where, now. They were sharp elbows jabbing her—one a little too hard, and then . . . There were corners and fingers and canes. They all wanted to kill her, and take Jim away from her and take away her love. That's what they all wanted!

Jodi stumbled a little and half-walked, half-ran across the blurred roomful of people, past them all and into the glinting bright, hot, white street.

It was almost time. Jim was always so punctual, he'd be there, waiting. But where was it? Where was she now?

Suddenly the black satin woman came up into her mind and floated there, like a trick movie effect. The camera moved into the woman's face, then into her black dark eyes, the eyes of a witch with mystic powers. *Moon in Gemini*—she'd said that. *Oh yes. I see a tragedy, a loss . . . something will happen . . .*

The light changed. Across the street with the people. Don't look at them, don't notice them. The other side: now, the long block, down the long block. Only a little distance now. They don't see me. I'm going too fast for them. Mark. Little Mark, help me, help me run!

Jodi ran and heard her heels click on the pavement. Heels—she shouldn't have worn them. Flat shoes, they'd told her, and her six months along. The heels would turn and she'd pitch into the street and the people would walk over her with their heavy crushing weight, kill her, kill Mark . . . no, Mark would be saved, and Mother Hilton would get him too.

It was already past twelve. The clock said so and the clock was always right. Past twelve. She wrapped her hands about the front of her dress and felt the breath flood in painfully slow, like small knives cutting at her insides, cutting a little deeper every time, trying to get deeper and deeper.

And then, with the flickering white and red turning to black in her mind, with her feeling the movement and the life seep from her, there, there ahead a few feet, was the door.

Through the door, into the sudden coolness and the sounds of sharp things. Rattling dishes, trays, glasses. People, hushed, looking at her, moving toward her to cut off the air.

Jodi fell into the booth, moved into the corner and let the tears come.

She didn't even feel the gentle hand on her shoulder, or hear the soft troubled voice.

"Jodi, honey. Jodi. Is anything the matter?"

The Indian Piper

First the heat took his courage. It went into his body not as it had gone into the ash bricks and soiled cement, but as a chill along his spine; coursing coldly to his heart, making his heart beat faster. The heat in the darkened room was the first to take his courage.

Then the smells came to make him tremble. The stale cookies, the bubbling fish-oils and the human odors suspended in the aqueous exhaust of nearby candy factories and held rigid in the air. The sound of feet upon carpetless floors, the buzz of a fly darting in quick circles; and the phalanx in the street below, dancing and shouting in muffled monotony. All the sounds and feelings of the living world, come suddenly to stop him.

And now, the Pipes. The mellow reedy notes issuing down the hallways and coming through Clayton's door, pulsing in the room and seeming almost to come from the room.

He turned his eyes from the red and yellow Saint and pulled back the safety catch of the revolver, deliberately. The steel against his temple was reassuring for a moment, but then it became cold, turning things over rapidly in his mind. The feel of the muzzle brought sudden images to Clayton, never shutting out the other, never stilling the Pipes, but clearly drawn. The jaded squib in the newspaper: ONE-TIME FABULOUS BIG-BUSINESS TYCOON, HARRY CLAYTON, COMMITS SUICIDE IN SHABBY EAST SIDE FLAT. And, of course, the photograph to go with it: the grotesquely crumpled body lying in a pool of gore and filth.

He smiled at the thoughts. Who could tell? They might even run a three-installment story on his career. That would sell papers, provided anyone remembered Harry Clayton after so many years. Though he knew a dozen people who would pay seven cents an issue for the story—at least a dozen. Even federal prisoners get to read . . .

Clayton shook his head and tried to concentrate. He re-

membered his boast of "pulling the shutters" on unwelcome
reflections and tried the trick now. But the heat and the smells
remained and the music of the Pipes was getting louder.

*Squeeze the trigger, boy, never pull it; you lose control when you pull
it.*

The thin reedy notes on the treble register squealed into the
room, vibrating the glass and the pieces of steel. He could feel
the note in the revolver, shaking the metal, making it hard to
hold. He clenched his finger about the curved trigger and pulled
slightly; the trigger moved a fraction of an inch but did not trip
the hammer. The gun was still cold on his temple and sweaty in
his hand, and now it became heavy and his arm was tired in its
awkward angle.

He sighed, tossed the gun into a damp mess of bedclothes and
walked to the closed window.

People danced in the street, men and women with bodies
pressed together, moving jerkily in the street and shouting. A
frail bandbox stood at the corner, supported by wood scraps;
men sat upon it with musical instruments to their mouths and
in their laps. A large man in a grey suit stood waving his hands
in front of the orchestra and looking tired. And in front of every
other store was posted a gaudily painted Saint with a benign
expression.

Clayton could hear the discordant melodies above the sounds
of voices and above the Pipes—harsh, unwelcome melodies that
reminded him of the past years, of the loneliness and the hate and
the bitterness he knew.

He slid back into the chair and closed his eyes. Sleep would
quiet it all and perhaps tomorrow he would find courage.

The Pipes exploded in his consciousness. The single notes,
unadorned, jumping or sliding from tone to tone, weaving complex fugues and simple airs, tearing even sleep from him. And
suddenly he became aware of them. Prison hadn't stopped his
logic and he began to wonder about the Pipes, why they both-
ered him so, why they made him feel as he did. He lit a cigarette,
walked to the sink to draw a glass of water and settled back in the
chair.

He would have gone through with it if it hadn't been for that crazy flute. He would have squeezed the trigger, the fragment of lead would have ripped through his skull and through the tender tissues of his brain and it would all have been over. But somehow, they had stopped him; they had caused him to be alert so he could not focus his attention on what he was doing. The sounds, he realized, meant something, something special, that got beneath his skin and rashed. It was almost, he thought, like the old feeling. But without logic, for they were just noises from a stick played by an old fool four doors down the hall.

The orchestra in the street had adjourned slowly, trailing off instrument by instrument until only the far-away voices remained. The other things left also; Clayton lit another cigarette and realized he was thinking now only of the Pipes.

All right. Tomorrow he would put the bullet through his head. But now, for a moment, he could summon Harry Clayton vestigially and figure the proposition. He could still do that, he could still be annoyed at things he didn't understand; and this was all he didn't understand, all in the world.

All right.

The brown man had come at night like a thief, quietly, while the hotel slept. No one knew where he had come from or what he did, or how he lived, for the room had been unfurnished and no one had heard the sound of trunks rumbling up the stale, decaying staircases. And that's all there was to it, until the following night when the music of the Pipes first began to fill the dirty halls. The single note, low, soft, and then from behind the door, other notes, slowly put one upon another and woven finally into lines of melody and harmony.

He looked like an Indian because of the beard and the immense turban on his head, but that didn't have to be true. He could be a man in paint or even a Negro from the Village, a musician, a mentalist, a screwball or a fake.

So, there's a brown man without any furniture sitting in a dingy room playing a flute till all hours.

Clayton rose and looked at himself in the mirror, grinned at the pale reflection. He thought of other brown men and certain promises he had made; but the memory was crushed in an instant, as pain is crushed by death.

The Indian, alone with his flute. The brown man who smiled at everybody but did not speak, who filled the rooms with music and drained the courage from suicidal fingers.

Clayton listened. The note this time was in the bass, wavering, fragile, like a china saucer or a woman's hair. It vibrated, then spiraled upwards to a clear constant tone and held to silence.

The brown man whom people feared and loved. He remembered—or thought he remembered, for nothing was clear now —that they were going to evict him because of the noise, then they didn't. The old woman in the room by the laundry closet had told him once that she had begun to like the music. They all did. They all loved the Piper.

They did; he could almost hear their words and see their faces. They did.

Clayton grinned and picked the revolver off the bed. He unlocked the door, eased the safety catch of the revolver back into place and walked into the hall.

The doors were all alike, with the exception of one; an artist had lived in that room, so the landlord said, and had one night painted the door bright colors. But the colors were faded now and were beginning to peel away to the rot beneath.

Clayton walked past the doors, past the room with the porcelain sign which read BATH and on to the end of the hallway. He stopped at the open window and looked over his shoulder. The straight walkway was empty; below, far distant in the street came the sounds of life, and from behind the doors muted voices. But he was alone.

He waited for a while, listening to the Pipes. They were louder than he had ever heard them, pulsing in the air, descending and ascending along their melodies. Clearer now, sadder, somehow, slower than before.

He hefted the gun in his pocket and rapped sharply upon the door.

There was no reaction. The melody continued, broke from

any refinements and stated itself with simple clarity. Clayton sensed that this had happened, that the music had suddenly begun a summation.

He rapped again, glancing back over his shoulder down the hall. What if someone should see him, what then? And why shouldn't someone see him, he wondered, aware that the music had come to a soft stop.

The door opened abruptly; it swung wide and the darkness of the room came into the hall.

An old man with dark brown skin stood in the doorway smiling. About the old man's head was a great turban, spotlessly white: the tassel fell over his shoulder. There was a long beard and mustache, edged with grey.

The old man said nothing.

Clayton extended his hand, and noticed the firm grip that met his.

"I hope I'm not disturbing you," he said.

"By no means, sir. I am so happy that you chose to visit me. Come in, won't you, come in."

Clayton walked by the bowed figure into the room and waited for the door to close.

"Now then, sir," said the old man, walking to the window and raising the shades. "I do hope that you've not come to complain about my music. That would make me very unhappy."

Clayton laughed.

"The other way around, Mr.—"

"Am. Mr. Am."

"Harry Clayton. No, Mr. Am, I certainly did not come to complain. In fact, I like your music so much that I finally decided I'd have to meet you."

The old man beamed. Light flaked into the room, and Clayton saw with a shock that there was no furniture. The room was bare, but for a wooden chest, which sat in a corner; only this and unconnected gas pipes and sockets without bulbs.

Mr. Am squatted down and motioned Clayton to join him.

"Isn't it strange, Mr. Clayton, that everyone should like the music! I had thought that perhaps there would be those who might object; consider my amazement at your compliment. Are you a musician, sir?"

"No, no, nothing like that. Don't care too much for it, actually. But there's something about those sounds that—well, it's hard to explain."

Mr. Am nodded his head. Then he gestured about the room.

"You must pardon the spare furnishings: I had not contemplated visitors. My own wants, as you can see, are not demanding."

Clayton looked around and then back at the old man. He spoke good English, didn't seem to be crazy. But what about food, and where did he sleep?

Already he missed the music. The outside noises were low now, but harsh, and he was returned to his reason for visiting the Indian Piper. It wasn't clear: only the flute. He had to see it, then logic would follow. But the hunch told him, ask to see the flute.

"Mr. Clayton, may I ask why you are not out in the street at this time, dancing with the people? It's a beautiful night for it and the orchestra is very good, all things considered."

"I was out for a while," he lied, "but it's too hot for parties."

"Ah, but this is special, I am told: a celebration to raise funds for the church, or something like that. At any rate," Mr. Am turned toward the closed window, "it is quite religious."

Clayton rose a bit and could see out the window. Black-haired men and women moved nervously, tiredly, their bodies looked close; and little children sat on curbstones, watching with wondrous eyes. He could see gaunt men with red faces standing back against stores, trembling. And for a moment the orchestra, which was playing loudly again, and the fetid odors came into the room.

"Too hot for parties," Clayton said.

"Well then, now that we've met, what shall we talk about?"

"I was thinking, Mr. Am, that maybe I could get you to play that flute for me."

"Why, of course, I should be glad to!"

The old man got up from the floor gracefully and went to the chest in the corner of the room.

"I generally keep it locked up, you see," he remarked, "because it is the one thing of value that I own."

Mr. Am took from a pocket a large key, which he inserted in the lock of the chest.

"However, almost any key opens the lock."

Mr. Am lifted a crumpled paper bag from the chest, carefully closed the lid and walked back to Clayton. He reached into the bag.

Clayton's heart began to pump the moment he saw it. He hadn't known exactly what to expect, perhaps an ordinary piccolo or a wooden stick, but—this! He realized that his mouth had opened, and now the logic formed swiftly in his brain. The reason he had come, the thoughts he had considered in his own room.

The old man held in his hands a slender shaft, perforated from tip to tip with gems and pearls and substances Clayton could barely guess at. In the middle, the shaft separated into four thinner prongs, each carved in gilt and woven between what appeared to be emeralds and sapphires. Everywhere the jewels seemed not merely affixed, but placed to form a design; it burned and flashed, but was delicate. It became the center of the room.

"Is it not a handsome thing?" Mr. Am asked.

Clayton swallowed and managed to look away. He struggled to keep composure in his voice.

"This is what you play the music on, is it?"

"Yes, these are the Pipes. Not quite the usual idea of what they should look like, I suppose; however . . ."

The old man put the instrument to his lips and immediately there issued a thin note that fell from one of the tips and mellowed into silence. Then other notes followed, singly stated at first, then combining into harmonies, with melody after melody predominating.

Clayton could not hear the music; he stared at the Pipes, solidifying the idea in his mind. He did not notice that Mr. Am had stopped playing the Pipes and was looking at him.

He fidgeted uneasily. "Please go on," he said.

Clayton watched the old man replace the instrument's reed,

saw the old fingers curl about the jewelled prongs. He tried iden-
tifying: there was a band of what could be nothing but pure gold,
at the fork of the prongs; and there were sapphires, amethysts,
great pearls and rubies that were the redness of blood. Unquestionably the object was worth a fortune; you didn't have to be
a lapidary to tell that, you had only to know the look of fakes.

Before him, what he had thought lost: the road back to the
old days. And he had made sure that no one had seen him in the
hall . . .

He would have to think carefully; talking would give him
time to think. The old man was senile, obviously, didn't know
what he had, or worse, didn't care. He would have to talk awhile.

"Mr. Am, what exactly is that called? I don't think I've ever
seen anything quite like it."

Mr. Am took the instrument from his lips once more and put
it in his lap.

"It is called by many names; in fact—and this is interesting
—almost everyone thinks of it in a different way. But we may
call it the Pipes."

"A beautiful thing, all right. Tell me, is it old, I mean, are
there many like it?"

The old man laughed loudly.

"Oh yes, indeed. There have been more imitations of it than
of anything else I can think of. They have all been spurious,
however; none has ever achieved precisely the tone."

"Why is that? You're not going to tell me it's the only one in
existence?"

"Exactly that, sir. There is a story behind its manufacture,
which perhaps you would care to hear—I see that you are taken
with the Pipes. Briefly, in antique times men of great wisdom
worked at one goal and one only: to produce the object you see
in my hands. For lifetimes and in many parts of the world they
toiled willfully—and it must be said that at times they came
quite close. But their experiments always ended poorly, they
were disappointed and died disappointed. For years all the great
wise men tried and failed, made pipes and thought that they
would be sweet and found them to be harsh and one with their

world, which they hated. Until it was thought by everyone that the Pipes would never be! The men gave up trying; they went back to their homes and lived in darkness.

"But then, to the consternation of one and all, sir, an old man whom none had suspected of special talents decided one day to climb a hill; and he climbed the hill up beyond the clouds and when he returned, he had with him the Pipes!"

Clayton heard only half of what Mr. Am was saying. He got the point of historical value, if there was anything at all in the story, even the hint of truth; but he rejected this idea. No, it would never do to take it to a large firm. There would be publicity and the red tape he once knew so well. Break it up and take it to pawn shops—not the nests along the Bowery, but the ones in the office buildings, where rich wives took their husbands' cufflinks.

"And he was doubted. The people listened to the music, heard the golden tones and doubted. So, the old man became angry and gave the Pipes to a thief. It has passed from that time to this by such men, who learned the Pipes, who wished only to play and be heard."

"You don't say!"

"Oh yes! So, you can see the strange value of the Pipes, can you not—the value apart from mundane considerations?"

"Yes, yes, that I can, Mr. Am."

The old man sighed and refolded his legs.

"The thing was," he said, "the people expected an instrument full of complex intricacies; when the greybeard returned with an art object which any simpleton could play, then no one believed."

"You say it's not hard to learn, then?" Clayton asked.

"By no means. One need only the honest desire to learn: the rest comes, you might say, by ear. Though the one consideration is of much importance. Here, you can see—there are only ten openings."

Mr. Am passed the Pipes to Clayton.

He felt the cool strength of an emerald upon one finger and looked down at a constellation of gems. He hesitated, then put the ebony reed to his lips and pushed a breath into it, remembering the sweetness of the melodies.

A wild, horrible screech suddenly echoed from the walls. Quickly, he pulled the Pipes from his face.

The old man smiled complacently.

"Mr. Clayton," he said slowly, "have you decided yet how you are going to go about stealing the Pipes from me?"

He had wasted too much time! Now he would have to act fast.

"What gave you such an idea?"

"The color in your cheeks, the bulge in your pocket. Or say that I am a mind-reader, if you choose. Whatever the case, I confess interest in what is to follow."

Clayton rose, feeling foolish and embarrassed. He thought of the tableau in his room a short time before, the picture of a pale thin man with a gun to his head, amid dirt and cheapness and . . .

He took the revolver from his pocket and pointed it at Mr. Am.

"Mr. Clayton, in prison you were acquainted with convicted murderers—did they strike you as a pleasant lot?"

"How did you know that?" Clayton snapped. "How did you know that I was—"

"I have seen other ex-convicts; I recognize the pallor and surely you must know that the suit is obvious."

"Then you know who I am?"

"I am well acquainted with your background, sir; in fact, I studied your career with much fascination from its beginning. You had great potentialities, Mr. Clayton, really great. The power of inducement, the power of persuasion, all the great things a man can wield, those you had in abundance. Many thought you would actually live up to your promises, that the world would indeed be a better place—"

"Shut up."

"I have no doubt that there are many who champion you even today, who insist you were wronged by the law, a martyr of a vicious political system."

"Stop it!"

The old man carefully placed the Pipes on the floor and pushed them toward Clayton.

"Well then, since you intend to shoot me in any event, surely you cannot object to a few questions from an old admirer. The orchestra has begun again in the street and no one would hear even if I were to scream. Oh yes, you have me entirely at your mercy; so let us chat just for a bit."

Clayton squatted on the floor, not knowing why. The power of the idea was gone and it remained fixed, so why shouldn't he listen? Here was someone at least who remembered him. He would do what he had to do: perhaps there was not such a hurry after all.

"If you know so much about me, there doesn't seem much to discuss."

"On the contrary! I must ask you some things that would otherwise bother me."

"You know I've got to kill you now that you've told me these things, don't you?"

"I suppose so."

"Then ask your questions."

"First, I should like you to go back eighteen years, to the day you received the inheritance. I should like you to examine the memory for a moment."

Clayton started to object, then found he could not check his mind; suddenly, as though commanded, it raced back. Only vaguely was he aware of where he was, of the gun in his hands.

He remembered.

"You had other ideas then, Mr. Clayton. You were going to take the money and buy yourself power, that is true. But do you recall what you were going to do with that power?"

The voice was distant, far . . . Clayton felt the stench of the wooden tenements and the brick kilns full of starving people; he saw the long lines of hungry men and screaming children and the young men suddenly made old and the leather rotting from their soles. He remembered.

He pulled his mind from the el, from the young man in the

el and from the tornado in the canyons of poverty that he had sworn he would not forget.

The old man's voice caught him before his finger could curl around the trigger.

"Now, Mr. Clayton, to the day you discovered the profound influence money could yield in all the hopeless wheels, when you realized that the achievement of your goal was not far distant. I will not move or call for help; I ask merely that you think of a few days, a few highlights in your history that the newspaper scribes somehow neglected. Think of yourself in the state capitol, with the strings depending from every finger, and of the lad in the elevated train on the south side of Chicago."

Clayton became frightened. He tried desperately to hold his mind to the present, but it went whirling back to images more vivid than his most vivid nightmares.

And the question he had avoided came to him now: what had happened? What had happened?

Then Clayton remembered the little Negro child sitting on the mound of rubbish, holding the whistle to his lips.

The little Negro child with the whistle and how beautiful the melodies were in the stagnant air; and how he had sworn.

The memories came rushing now, even as the old man talked. How he had kept promising and losing faith in the promises, losing interest, growing hard.

"You're crazy," Clayton shouted. "You're just trying to talk your way out of something. The answer to all my little worries is sitting right there beside you."

With effort he pulled the gun into position.

"My bargain was taken," said Mr. Am, "and you answered the questions the best you could. So then proceed with what you have to do."

Clayton gripped the gun firmly and held it at the old man's stomach.

His mind was a kaleidoscope of memories.

He would never give up and put a bullet through his head because he had failed once. No, of course not, that wasn't Harry Clayton. But that is what he had almost done, a few hours ago, less time, less! So why had he taken the little money they had given him and bought a revolver; why had he come to this dirty building and sat for nights listening to fantastic music?

Damn the crazy old man for making him remember, for showing him what he'd tried so hard not to recognize!

"Is it really too late?" Mr. Am was saying. "Is it? Now that you know, is it too late?"

"Of course it is!" Clayton screamed. "Yes! Yes!"

The memories came like sharp needles into his brain, things he had hidden, moulding and shaping themselves into patterns. Into answers.

The old man held something out to Clayton.

He looked down. In Mr. Am's hands was a battered shaft of tin, the peppermint colors faded and the one indentation bent in the middle. Then it was once more the jewelled treasure.

The old man rose to his feet and straightened his back. He did not smile.

Clayton stifled the sobs in his throat and clutched the Pipes to his body.

"I could not force you to come to me," the old man said, "and I could not make you listen. But you did come and you listened."

Clayton felt the strong hands beneath his shoulders, pulling him erect.

They walked to the window. Below, the street was empty; dim lights fell upon gutter-waste and picked out the colors painted upon the faces of the plaster Saints.

The old man put the Pipes to Clayton's lips and adjusted his fingers about the openings.

"It will take time and at first be very hard, but you will learn now."

Before the blackness entered his mind, Clayton heard the one clear note sing into the dark room—

The same dark room that was empty when he ran to it later, searching for the Indian Piper.

Lachrymosa

The little woman with the orange hair made her way through the rows of tombstones with a brisk step and an expression of infinite sadness upon her face. Past the tall stones and large onyx monuments she walked quickly, but by the less ornate reminders of man's fragile mortality, the little woman paused. Here she would sigh, right an overturned vase, remove a withered flower or take from her bouquet one yellow rose and drop it tenderly to the earth.

When she reached the plot at the north end of the cemetery, the little woman stood very still for a long time, clutching the roses to her bosom and silently regarding the three graves before her. Then she sighed deeply and distributed the flowers upon the graves.

The monuments were identical. Of pale white stone, smooth on the front and each topped with a figure of Cupid, they were spotless and suggested eternity. Upon the first was the inscription:

GUSTAV HALSTEAD

1897-1948

"A Good Man"

upon the second:

JOHN JACOB FOGARTY

1889-1950

"A Good Man"

and upon the third:

ALONZO HUMPHRIES

1890-1951

"A Good Man"

The third was the most recently chiseled, but, like the others, after the Roman manner.

The little woman shifted her silver fox furpiece so that the head, with its tiny staring eyes, dangled from her arm. With this arm she reached out and stroked consecutively the heads of the granite Cupids.

When the gentleman standing in the plot directly across straightened his shoulders and replaced his hat, the little woman with the orange hair said, "Such a good man."

The gentleman turned his head.

"I beg pardon," he said, "but were you speaking to me, madam?"

"What? Oh, oh, I'm so sorry. I didn't realize—It's just that —just that—" and with this the little woman put a hand to her head, veered uncertainly and slumped against the third tombstone. The gentleman in the next plot stared briefly, flushed and hurried to be of assistance.

"My dear woman, what's the matter? Here, my arm."

The little woman shifted her weight and breathed heavily for a space. Then she smiled.

"Silly of me," she said. "Only there are times when I suddenly feel so lost in this lonely place, so without hope."

The gentleman said, "I understand."

"All of a sudden I just went weak. I'm sorry you were troubled. I meant to trouble no one."

"Not a bit of it! When I saw you fall I was afraid, well, that you were distressed or ill. People do that sort of thing here; sometimes have to be carried off. But you're all right now?"

"It was good of you. Yes, I believe so. Merely a woman's weakness."

The gentleman said, "I understand" for a second time and glanced at the nearest grave.

"Oh. Some relative, or friend—?" he asked.

"If only it were!" cried the little woman. "That is, it is much worse. Lying deceased, there in the cold ground, is my late husband, Alonzo Humphries, may the good Lord bless and take his sweet soul." She clutched once more for support.

"Honestly?"

"Only six months ago I had Alonzo to help and guide me. Only six months. And now——"

They stood in silence as twilight crept upon all the tombstones and birds sang doleful melodies.

"My name is Smythe," said the gentleman, "Mordecai Smythe. I do hope you don't take offense at my interest."

Mrs. Humphries bit her lower lip and fell in a spasm upon the chest of Mr. Smythe, who, being a small man, was obliged to brace his heels in unnaturally soft earth. He held the sobbing woman.

Then Mrs. Humphries regained her strength.

"But you," she said, brokenly, "you too must be bereaved."

"Yes, yes, I'm afraid that's true. Over there," he gestured, "is my late wife, Addie, a help and a joy to me for many years."

"Oh dear, oh dear, you poor man. We sometimes forget that others share our unhappiness, don't we? You must be terribly hurt."

"Twelve years ago," said Mr. Smythe, gazing off into the mist, "she left me. But I come here every day; stay for hours and hours." He paused. "I've been here since noon. Somehow, I find that it's a help. I suppose, Mrs. Humphries, you think that a foolish idea of an old man?"

"No, indeed not. I think it's very inspiring. Why, you must even go without lunch!"

"Yes. You see, Addie passed on during lunch and—I have not been really hungry since."

"I'm sorry. Oh, people don't seem to feel the same way nowadays. Haven't you noticed it, Mr. Smythe?"

"I certainly——"

"I mean, marriage has taken on a new form in this modern world. It may be old fashioned of me, but I have always felt there is something sacred in marriage, something not even death could completely break asunder. It was the way Alonzo felt."

"You were married a long time?"

"In years, in this mortal plane? No, Mr. Smythe, not a long time in that sense. But in the spiritual sense, my late husband and I were joined since the very beginning."

Mr. Smythe took his hand quickly from Mrs. Humphries' shoulder. She swayed.

"You're right," he said, bitterly. "It means nothing to people nowadays. Live or die, it's all the same. They say, You must go on, and they can't understand why you don't. Do you know, you've been the first person I've met who's seemed to understand why I should want to come here every day!"

"I understand because I try to come as frequently myself. Often I have seen you, Mr. Smythe, and wanted somehow to comfort you."

"*You* have wanted to help *me*? Oh, Mrs. Humphries, oh, my good woman. . . ."

"Grief is a lonely thing."

"And you actually come every day?"

"Yes. I also have my reasons."

"No one, absolutely no one has been able to understand. They tell me I'm getting old, they tell me I shouldn't come to the cemetery."

"Perhaps," suggested Mrs. Humphries, "these other people have never known the fullness of love."

Mr. Smythe thumped his umbrella on the ground.

"Of course, of course, that's it! The fullness of love! Why, they've all forgotten the meaning of the word."

A thin rain began to fall in silver drops upon the cemetery. The two were alone, or as alone as it is possible to be in such a place, and they spoke in hushed tones, full of respect.

A drop of rain fell upon Mr. Smythe's nose and he opened his umbrella. In so doing he glanced at the other headstones upon whose mounds he was standing.

"Your family plot?" he asked.

"Yes," said Mrs. Humphries, simply.

"We'd better get on. That is, you might catch cold or something, here like this. Have you a car?"

Mrs. Humphries pointed across the tombs.

"Then, if it wouldn't seem rude, since it *is* raining, I mean—"

"Mr. Smythe, I would greatly appreciate the shelter of your umbrella to my car."

They descended from the graves and walked slowly alongside a row of eucalyptus trees.

"It's such a shame, in a way, Mr. Smythe. You should eat lunch and take care of yourself. Wouldn't—wouldn't *she* have wanted it that way?"

"Addie did so many things for me, I've fallen out of a lot since then. What does a retired businessman do, Mrs. Humphries, when he has lost his beacon?"

"I know, I know."

"Just aimless wandering, aimless, lonely wandering."

"Lonely."

"No one to understand, no one to turn to."

"I know."

"May I ask," said Mr. Smythe, stopping, "was it easy with your husband? I mean to say, his last moments were not painful?"

"Alonzo went quietly from this world."

"Heart trouble?"

"Well, no," corrected Mrs. Humphries, "not exactly that. Poison in his system. He was never a well man."

"Ah yes, I see. It was not so with me. Poor Addie took convulsions. It was horrible—during lunch, you know."

"How awful for you. What a great deal you have borne, Mr. Smythe!"

"Most other people don't seem to think so. Say it happens every day."

Mrs. Humphries edged closer in upon the umbrella.

"For me," she said, "it's like being taken and thrown into a dark pit. Alonzo was somewhat older than myself—oh, I knew it, but I had always wanted a mature man—and because of this I suppose I should have been prepared. But we're never prepared, never, are we! He used to say to me, 'Effie,' he would say, 'Effie, you are a fine woman and I was more than lucky to get you. But you must start thinking about afterwards. You must live when I am gone, for you have many good years ahead of you.' He used to tell me how lost he was before he met me, how I'd helped and aided him . . . But to go on *now*, with Alonzo sleeping under this very ground . . ."

Mrs. Humphries applied a handkerchief to her face and they were obliged to stop once more.

"Your husband said these things to you?" Mr. Smythe asked, as the walk was resumed. "Addie never put it quite like that."

"Alonzo was a good man."

"And he told you to go on, to live and things like that?"

"He did. Poor soul, he never realized how few people there are in the world with whom one could ever be really close. Close as a man and woman in love are."

Mr. Smythe clenched his teeth tightly and his stride became brisker.

"I never knew anyone else felt that way. It's how I feel; it's why I have to come here every day."

"Oh, but is there another life anywhere in this lonely world, for people like *us*, Mr. Smythe? I try, I *want* to think there is. But it's hard, so very hard, when one feels so alone."

Mr. Smythe opened his mouth to reply when his foot caught on a little wooden cross.

"Yes," he said, finding his balance, "that's true."

The rain thickened and the moon shone faintly through black clouds.

"Well, this is the drivepath. Is that your car?"

"Yes. A gift from Alonzo."

Mrs. Humphries unlocked the door of the large black Cadillac and slid gracefully behind the steering wheel.

"He used to drive it all the time," she said. "I don't do it so well, I'm afraid. But I'm going to have to learn a lot of things now, aren't I?"

Mr. Smythe accepted the gloved hand and shook it vigorously.

"You—you've been a consolation," he mumbled, "the day being so gloomy and all."

"And you helped me. I'll remember your help and your understanding."

Mr. Smythe continued to shake the hand that had somehow remained in his own. "Yes . . . well, ah, thank you," he said.

Mrs. Humphries pushed back a strand of her orange hair,

flung the silver fox furpiece about her neck and turned on the ignition of the Cadillac.

"We are two very lonely people, Mr. Smythe."

"Yes, aren't we, though. Perhaps—perhaps I will see you here again some time?"

"Perhaps. Seek strength in God, as I do. She would have wanted it like that. Goodbye."

"Remarkable. Remarkable."

Mrs. Humphries looked toward the dark-shrouded cemetery where, outlined dimly against the moon, could be seen three identical graves. She sighed and released the emergency brake.

Mr. Smythe bowed stiffly. "A man can be rich and own the earth," he remarked, "and still be alone. Goodbye."

He pulled his hat down tighter over his bald head and gestured with his umbrella. A black limousine rolled into sight.

Slowly the old gentleman walked toward the limousine.

"Oh, Mr. Smythe!"

He turned.

"Do you happen to like fried chicken?"

The Rival

Ryan Publications, Inc., glared impatiently at the elevator door, hit it once with his fist, and started up the stairs. His face was a composition in red. When he saw a reflection of it in the second-landing mirror, he paused. Easy, he told himself. Calm. Whatever you do, don't let her see that you're angry. Hurt, yes. Disappointed. *But not angry!*

He waited for his heart to stop hammering, then he straightened his tie, turned, and walked to the door.

No hint, now, he thought, as he entered the huge, modernistic living room. Let her hang herself.

"Tim?"

He resisted the impulse to ask who else she would be expecting at seven p.m. "Yeah."

"Be out in a sec!"

He tossed his hat onto the white leather couch and went to the bar and poured himself a double-Scotch. No question about it, he thought, downing half the glass. Her voice is dripping with guilt. Right now, she's in there, biting her lip, wondering—

He froze as a new thought came into his mind. Ann would never run such a risk, he told himself; yet, he would never have believed the other story, either, if he hadn't been given proof. Slowly, his eyes began to rove the room. At the closet, they paused.

He walked silently across the thick pile rug and opened the door. Almost at once he saw the coat. A brown-and-white check, faded and threadbare.

Again his heart began to hammer, only this time he could not control it. *Right in my own apartment!* he thought, trying not to believe what his reason told him. *And*—he looked again at the coat—*with a bum, at that!*

He gulped the rest of the Scotch and walked to the bathroom door. The shower was going full blast, and he could hear Ann humming.

Maybe, he thought, catching sight of the bedroom, he's here now. Hiding. Why not? I wasn't supposed to be home until midnight; she knew that. The coat's still there in the closet . . .

Forcing the sordid picture from his mind, Ryan made an exploratory trip. He was on his hands and knees, peering under the bed when Ann's voice said: "Did you lose your cuff-links again, darling?"

He jumped to his feet. "Yes," he said.

"Find them?"

"No."

Ann stood in the doorway, clad in a fluffy pink bath towel. Smiling, she walked to Ryan and kissed him gently on the cheek; then she began to dress.

"You're home early," she said. "Forget something?"

Ryan shook his head. "No," he said, "as a matter of fact, I didn't. I just decided to come home early. Anything wrong with that?"

"Just a little surprising, is all."

"I imagine so." He let the comment hang in the air for a moment, then, when it had dissipated, he turned toward the window. "I—thought we might make an evening of it," he said, carefully.

There was a short silence. Then: "Gosh, honey, that would be wonderful. But I promised Judy I'd go with her to that travel lecture tonight. You know, the one on Siam. She's made plans and everything. You do understand, don't you, dear?"

Ryan faced his wife. She was pulling on a sleeveless blue evening gown. "I understand," he said, tightly, "that you're a liar."

Ann stopped, her hands still behind her back, her fingers on the zipper of the dress. "What?" she said, in a small, still voice.

"I said that you're a liar. No doubt you did make an appointment tonight, but it wasn't with Judy Hunter, and it wasn't for a travel lecture. Neither were those other engagements."

"What's the matter with you, Tim? What are you talking about?"

Ryan felt the anger slide away, to be replaced by a heavy sadness. "Drop the act," he said. "I ran into Fred Hunter at lunch today. He told me he hadn't seen you for three months."

"Tim, I—"

"He said Judy's been down with a cold since last Saturday; hasn't been out of the house."

Ann bit her lip, the way she did whenever she was confused, but she did not speak.

Ryan took a step toward her. "There's someone else, isn't there?" he said. "You might as well tell the truth. It won't make any difference now."

Slowly, Ann nodded.

Ryan sighed. He felt betrayed, cheated—after all, hadn't he slaved day and night for years, building a small trade magazine business into a veritable publishing empire, for her, for them? —but, mostly, he felt hurt.

"Do you love him?"

"Yes."

"Who is he? Someone I know?"

Ann whispered, "Not exactly. You used to, though."

"I did?"

She nodded. "A long time ago."

Ryan searched his mind, frantically. Bob Stevens? No; Bob was in Cleveland. Dave Mundt? Ridiculous.

"Who?"

Ann paused, got a small handkerchief from the bureau drawer and touched her eyes. Looking at her, Ryan realized, suddenly, that she was still young and beautiful, just as she'd been when they were married. Everything seemed new to him.

"Would you like to meet him, Tim?"

He started to say, "No!" but that, he saw, would be admitting utter defeat. It was neither adult nor modern. "Why not?" he said, bitterly. "We could settle the whole thing. Besides, we have a lot in common already."

"No," Ann said, looking at him, "that isn't really true." She turned, and her tone changed to one of crisp efficiency. "Zip me up, darling. And hurry. I'm late as it is."

They rode in silence down the twisting boulevard, Ryan driving much faster than he usually did. After a half-hour he said, "Where now?"

"Keep going," Ann said. "When you get to the beach highway, turn right. I'll tell you from there."

Again, silence. The air turned cold as they approached the beach and Ryan rolled up his window. "This guy," he said, trying to keep his voice twentieth-century, "What's he like?"

"Oh," Ann said, "young. Sort of loud and—well, enthusiastic. You may not approve."

"Good looking, I suppose?"

"Yes. Very."

"Not too successful, though," he said, recalling the worn coat.

"Not in your way."

Ryan laughed.

"But he has a lot of good ideas!"

"I wouldn't be surprised." The big Lincoln shot through a tunnel. "This," Ryan said, "isn't any of my business, I guess, and it doesn't make any difference, but as a matter of interest, have you—"

"Several times," Ann said, emphatically.

Ryan scowled, pressed down the accelerator and skidded around a 30-mile-an-hour turn at 50. On the beach highway, he slowed to a more reasonable speed. To the left, the ocean moved like a dark blanket. He looked at it as he drove and was vaguely aware that he'd not been here for over five years.

The traffic thinned and soon they were approaching the hills of Malibu.

"Slow down," Ann said. Then she pointed. "There."

"There?" Ryan's mouth opened slightly.

"That's right."

He stopped the car and blinked. "The night," he said, "is full of surprises. I must say that I didn't expect your rendezvous to be a cheap motel on the beach!"

Ann looked at him and shrugged. "We like it," she said, and opened the door.

Fighting desperately for control, Ryan followed his wife

through the bamboo door into a stale, dimly-lit hallway, down the hallway to another door. It was labeled: "The Zebra Room."

As Ann removed a key and inserted it into the lock, he cleared his throat and said, "Hadn't you better go in first and explain? I wouldn't want him to have a heart attack."

"You're right. Wait here and I'll call when I'm ready."

The door opened and closed. Ryan stole a surreptitious glance back down the hall. There was something about the place, something— He thought of running outside and driving away, but that, of course, wouldn't do. Not for a man in his position. No: he'd have to face the fellow (any moment now) and act the way the head of a publishing chain ought to act in such a situation. Cool, reserved, haughty, casual.

"All right, Tim. You can come in."

Ryan's heart flopped over painfully. His hand trembled as he reached for the knob.

"Tim?"

He pushed the door forward and walked into the room. It was in semi-darkness, lit only by a small lamp in the corner.

"Where are you?" he muttered.

"Here."

He turned his head. Ann was lying on an immense bed, next to the picture-window. The covers were pulled aside. She had on a short black nightgown, nothing more. The moon drenched her in soft light. Beyond, there was the sea.

Ryan made an angry sound. He wheeled and snapped on the wall-switch and looked around the room. "Where is he?" he demanded.

"Right here," Ann said.

"I don't see him. What kind of a filthy joke—"

"Tim, if you want to see him . . . turn around."

Ryan glared for a moment, trying to fathom the peculiar expression in his wife's eyes; then, slowly, he turned.

And faced a mirror.

"Do you recognize him?"

In a flash, Ryan remembered. He remembered the room, this room, where he and Ann had spent their wedding night; the drive they'd taken down Sunset, along the beach, so many years ago, on a night like this, cool and windy, with the moon shining and the ocean moving like a dark blanket—he remembered the old coat he'd worn then . . .

"Do you know who your rival is now?" Ann asked, stepping into the reflection.

"Yes."

"And—you won't stand in our way?"

"No, darling. I won't stand in your way."

Ryan Publications, Inc., snapped off the light and held his wife close and kissed her. Then, together, they walked back toward the bed.

The Junemoon Spoon

I'd been trying to push a brand of corsets to the big department stores, and the luck I was having, you'd think women didn't have stomachs anymore. When I pulled into town I'd made expenses and just about enough for a couple drinks at Frank and Eddie's. So that's where I went and that's what I had.

The usual bunch was there. Frank Wilmszyk was the only one who looked happy so I figured they'd all run up against the same thing. That's the way it is, once in a while. Sometimes you make a big killing in one place, then you go somewheres else with the identical same merchandise and nobody's interested. You can talk yourself hoarse and smile till you think your teeth are going to drop out, but there's never anybody home. They're always "Sorry, we're quite busy now." It's the breaks. You expect them and so you figure them. But even though you've made a little ash to go on, you still don't feel so wonderful when it happens. It's like winning twenty hands of poker and then losing fifteen. I don't know why, but you're never happy about the twenty you won. Instead you cry about losing, even if you're dough ahead. That's life, if you know what I mean.

So anyway, I sat down in a corner all prepared to spend a nice evening crying in my beer. Fred looked around and decided this owl-eyed bunch was not for him, so he left. All the others moaned around like me, not talking and staring off into space. Eddie went over to the juke and put on Hearts and Flowers, but nobody laughed this time.

The last person in the world I wanted to see was Harry Jackson. So, naturally, that's who walked in. Not that Harry doesn't have personality—but that he's got too much. A salesman with too much personality is like a preacher with a megaphone. You get the donations all right, but you don't make many friends.

Well, you picture a guy who could talk Jane Russell into buying a barrel of bust developer and who once sold a carton of

Bibles to Joe Dominic's gang and you've got Harry Jackson right to a T. You'd be impressed, if you know what I mean, but you wouldn't like him. You'd get the feeling he's trying to sell you something the minute he shakes your hand. And you'd be right.

But I've got to say, Harry could have fooled me this time, if I didn't look close.

It wasn't the same fellow I'd known for seven years. No warwhoop, no calls to set everybody up. He just walked in, quiet-like, and ordered a drink. It could have been Cardinal Spellman.

I was too miserable to try and duck. I looked into my drink, making like I didn't notice anybody, but of course Harry spotted me. He sat down at the table slow and tired.

He took a big gulp of whatever he was drinking and said, "Hiya, Bernie."

I said hiya back and that seemed like the end of the conversation.

Harry sat for a while, doodling his fingers in his glass, and then he let out a sigh that made everybody look up. And more sighs and more doodling. It made me nervous and I wasn't feeling so good anyway.

And besides, this didn't make sense. Harry had been gone quite a while and whenever that happened, you could lay money that he'd come back with a yard-wide smirk and a pocket full of the old redeemer. Instead, he looked like Joe Louis right after that fight with Charles. He ordered two more of what he had, and then started to balance match sticks on the sides of the glass. By this time I was getting a headache.

I said to him, "What's the matter, Hot-Shot—you only make two grand this trip?"

He looked very sad.

"Cut it out, Bernie."

And so we just sat there. This was new, all right. But I was still too interested in my own hard luck to pry into anybody else's. Couple hours and ten beers later most of the others had cleared out, but Harry didn't look like he was going anywheres. A guy who'd won the sweepstakes and lost his ticket couldn't look sadder than Harry looked. Black and dismal, like a fish.

Finally, he lifted up his head. The careful, slow way he did it, I could tell he had a pip on already.

"Bernie," he said to me, "what kind of justice is there in this crummy world?"

Coming from a guy like Harry, this was not the type of question you'd answer in a hurry.

"All kinds," I said. "Depends on how you look at it."

Noncommittal, if you know what I mean.

He shook his head and then grabbed hold of it.

"No, there isn't. There isn't any. Not a lousy bit of it. None."

"What are you talking about, chum? Don't tell me Harry Jackson hasn't made a killing!"

He looked over his shoulder to be sure the place wasn't jammed. Then he ordered a few more from Eddie—a couple for me and a couple for himself—and settled back. I saw what was coming as I started to leave. But he pulled me back down.

"Bernie, I'll tell you about it. I wouldn't tell anybody but you, because you're my pal. None of these other crummy bums—just you."

I saw it wasn't any use. Always the same. The story how he dumped a carload of stuff none of the rest of the world would look at, off on the biggest store in the state. Not the kind of thing you want to listen to right after you miss the boat on something that's ducksoup to push like corsets.

But what can you do?

"Right after I got rid of that load of pimple removers," Harry began, "I decided it would be nice to travel. So I asked myself, where haven't you been? The South. I hadn't ever been south of Chicago. So what does Harry Jackson do?"—*that's the way he talks, like Harry Jackson was somebody else*—"He gets himself a travel folder and starts to get ready. Monaghan, over at the warehouse, was having trouble with those stinkin' vitamin pills and skin jellies, so he asks me to take them over for him, at one-third our cost. Pretty good? What do I do? I get them and ease him down to one-fourth our price."

I knew what he was talking about. Izzie Monaghan had gotten himself stuck with a 'house full of surplus "health" stuff that wouldn't go at all, even in a market crying for the junk. Those pills, I personally knew, would eat the stomach out of a crowbar. And the skin jellies would finish the job.

Well, (Harry went on) I throw the slop in the trailer and in a few days I'm breezing along toward points Soof. With the cash-money I picked up on the last job I could afford to take my time —you know, stop in for a mint julep and chew the lip with the peasants—but is that Harry Jackson? Business first, I always said. Business first. Save the palaver for when you got nothing left to push.

Bessie conked out only once and in less than a week I was right in the heart of Alabama. And here, I said to myself, is where I really clean up! Talk about pickings—why nobody branched out in that direction is something I couldn't understand. It would be like taking candy from a brat.

First thing I did was find me a nice, respectable town. The big ones were okay, but that takes a little work. Big towns are pretty much all alike. So I drove through Montgomery, kind of look-ing her over, and stopped at a likely burg called Mobile.

I'm telling you, Bernie, nothing could have been sweeter. The way those people shuffled around, like they didn't care what hap-pened, and the big open-arm pitch they heaved was enough to do the old Jackson heart plenty good. I got myself installed in a place called the Battle House—an old dump but strictly class— and unloaded most of the merchandise in the room. It was settle back and rake it in.

They didn't have many little vitamin shops, like in L.A., but the drugstores were all run by old women. Need I say more, need I say more? The business suit, the genteel line, the medical en-dorsements—one, two, three, and it was in the bag.

Well, this lasted for a while, but pretty soon I run out of stores. And I was getting ready to shove when the hotel manager told me about a couple little towns nearby that made real nice visiting.

Now Harry Jackson isn't the type, so I don't need to tell you, who likes to sit around in some two-bit burg. But, I don't know, there was something that told me to stay put. I'd stocked nine-tenths of the drug stores with Philpott's Miracle Vitamin and Dr. Wunder's Skin Jelly, with a rake-in of almost a 0, and if there was a riding distance to some place where I could dump the rest, I didn't figure on pulling out. I knew I couldn't stay much longer, because people would start using that poison, but I figured a few days wouldn't make much difference. So I paid for another week and got the directions to those little towns.

The first one—believe it or not—was called Vinegar Bend. It wasn't too big, but awful, awful nice. When I got through there, all I had left was a suitcase of the jellies. And by that time I was itching to get back to L.A., so I pushed Bessie out from the Battle House the next day for that second town. I was sure I could clean up.

This other fleatrap was called Sneadville. Few drugstores, one or two theaters—you know. It was about a hundred miles from Mobile, so I decided to spend the night and start out fresh the next day. The hotels were all crummy, but I found one that was half-way decent. Not the Roosevelt, but it had clean sheets.

It looked like a cinch. Just a lazy, happy little joint with just the right amount of loose money floating around. The people dressed like it was 1851 instead of 19 and they looked so dumb I was surprised that they could talk.

Well, there I was, an honest salesman trying to drum up a little business with my merchandise, see, that's all. Trying to make a living, like anybody else. And here's what happens.

I'm not sleepy and besides, it's too early to go to bed, so I decide to walk around and take in a little of the local scenery. The hotel was big and stood out like a sore thumb, so I knew I wouldn't get lost.

So I walked around for a while, looking for a cocktail bar —and you'd think it was prohibition from how many I found. Closest thing to a saloon was a joint called "The Spa" and it was nothing more than a reconditioned hash-house. But, like I said, it was early and the old throat was parched, and I decided to give the dump a try.

There weren't many people in it. A corny song was going on

the juke and a couple of old birds were lipping it over in a corner. Oh, they were friendly—don't get me wrong. Just not my type, if you get me. I didn't know anything about ham hocks and red-eyed peas, so I got a beer and ambled over to a table. About this time a grizzled old guy looks over, grins like a mule and heels it to my spot, carrying a chair with him.

I wasn't feeling unsociable or anything, but you know how it is, Bernie, when you kind of enjoy being by yourself. I made like I didn't see him. The old guy doesn't notice this and, wheezing like a boiler, he plumps himself down next to me. What do I do? I nod and smile.

After all, he might own the biggest drugstore in town. And if you're a salesman you've got to be pleasant to everybody, but *everybody*.

So anyway, this gazabo sits down and pours half of my beer into his glass.

"Well, young feller," he says to me, "so you're the salesman just got in town?"

You don't know these little Alabama towns, Bernie. They're murder on knowing everything about what's going on. How the old guy found out about me, I couldn't say. Probably the hotel proprietor. Oh, they got ways, all right. Like for instance, he knew my name. It isn't so unusual, because I'd given the hotel clerk my card, but even so it gives you a creepy feeling to hear people you don't know calling you by your name.

He talked with a mouthful of mush, all full of y'all's and heah's. You know, the Yassuh business. And I smiled and told him I liked Sneadville and might make it my home some day.

Then, all of a sudden, he asks me, "What are ya sellin', son?" And naturally, Harry Jackson doesn't have to be hit over the head to see a good thing. The old boy was practically holding out his money.

"Well, sir," I said, "I take it that you are familiar with the famous Dr. Wunder?"

When he nodded his head yes I knew this was it. Maybe Sam Ingall wasn't so dumb when he tagged that phony monicker on his muck.

"Dr. Wunder has developed a miraculous skin jelly, sir, which he does not wish to cheapen by vulgar advertising. He has therefore chosen to send out selected representatives to practically give the people his revolutionary discovery. It has been enjoying such a success that I'm afraid it will be six months before even the back orders can be filled."

The old guy's eyes brighten and I see that another jerk that I didn't notice before is listening to our conversation. A mean-looking, dark-haired number, but he looked interested as I talked in a louder voice.

"You see, sir, Dr. Wunder's Famous Skin Jelly has the power to transform your flesh to the bloom of youth. Goodbye wrinkles, goodbye unsightly eruptions! Although the price will be increased, due to difficulties in obtaining certain of the extracts, it has been selling for four dollars a large, eight ounce bottle."

The old bird asked to see a sample and, luckily, I had one with me. Always carry a sample, I used to say—even when you go to bed. He looked the junk over for a long time, sniffed around and finally asked the question.

"Son, do you suppose I might get a bottle of this? It'd sure surprise the wife!"

I hemmed and hawed about back orders for a while, then agreed to let him have the sample for five bucks. Which was still a buck over what I had been charging, and, believe me, I could have kicked myself when I thought that I could have been getting this much! He took the stuff, chuckled around a while, dabbed fingerfulls of it on his hands right then and there, and sat back like he expected something to happen. It was hard, Bernie, to keep from laughing in his face.

Just as I was feeling good and getting ready to interview the hairy job who kept ankling around, the door opens and in steps a dame who—Bernie, trust my word—a babe who is stacked, but stacked, like nothing Harry Jackson had ever seen before. She looked like a cross between Daisy Mae and Hedy Lamarr, dressed in a ratty gunnysack affair that clung around those curves like it was wet.

Bernie, you know me. Harry Jackson's been around. I know a sharp piece of material and take it from me, this was first class merchandise. When she walked there wasn't anything that didn't jiggle a little bit on her, and that luscious blonde hair came practically down to her waist, clinging around. It was a sight for sore eyes, Bernie, and my eyes weren't sore!

The strange thing was that this dish was all alone. She walked in, looks nice at everybody in the place and orders a glass of milk from the barkeep.

Old Hamfat next to me hollers, "Hello, Julie girl," and the dish waves back, looking everywhere but at me. I naturally get more than interested.

But when I start to get up and excuse myself, gristlebeard pulls me down. Then he points over at the dark-haired number as if that explained everything. I tried again but the same thing happened. Then the big, mean, ugly guy takes something out of his pocket (I noticed that it was wrapped in cotton) and ambles over to where Gorgeous is sitting. I bet I glared holes through old bird next to me. But he chuckles away like Boris Karloff, maneuvering his chair closer to mine. Then he bends down till his mouth is flapping over my ear, and whispers: "That's Julie Patterson, old Colonel Patterson's granddaughter. She's a goner tonight."

"What do you mean, a goner," I asked him.

"Just that, boy. A goner. Clem got the spoon this time."

I figured the old boy for a looney, but it burned me to see that ignorant jerk steal the march on me. So I asked Grandpa what he was talking about. The girl was facing me, over there on the opposite side of the room, and Lon Chaney with the beard was honeying her up. When she smiled her teeth were the whitest I'd ever seen, and her mouth kind of crinkled at the sides. When I looked down and saw she didn't have any shoes or stockings, brother, that blew the whistle.

"Are you speaking about that very attractive young girl in the corner?"

"Sure I am, son—who else would I be talking about? You seen her, the second she opened the door. But t'won't do ya no good, 'cause she's a goner. For tonight, anyway. Clem must've rented the spoon."

"Clem, I imagine, is the fellow seated with the young lady?"

"You imagine right, young feller. Ugly hound, ain't he!"

The old boy was right. That guy Clem was one of the biggest, stupidest-looking yokels I'd seen in quite a while. But the way she looked at him you'd think he was Clark Gable. I mean, Bernie, that was a disturbing thing to have happen—especially to Harry Jackson. The longer I sat there looking at her, the more appealing life got. She didn't bat an eye, though. Just went on grinning and gushing over this other guy—and he leaned back like it was in the bag. Then I saw him take the wrapping off his little package. It was nothing but a dirty wooden spoon, the kind Phil sports at his bistro.

The old fella pulls my ear over again and wheezes, "That's it. They'll be leaving soon, you watch."

And sure enough, the second the babe pipes this piece of equipment, she looks like she's going to faint. Buster gets up, flings a buck or so to the barkeep, and in three seconds they're out the door. From the window I could see him put his arm around her waist—and she didn't look like she cared one little bit.

Bernie, you don't know how screwy that looked. The big guy was uglier than the Swedish Angel, with more hair than a gorilla. And yet he picks up that gorgeous job in ten minutes flat. And all the while, he's waving this filthy spoon around like it was a wand or something.

The old boy kept on chuckling and he could see I was interested.

"That's the first time I've seen the spoon for twenty, thirty years. The Hermit said he'd never rent it out, after what happened 'tween Jake Spiker and that politician's daughter. Clem must have talked him into it."

"I don't exactly understand you, sir," I said. "Do you mean that young lady was not acquainted with the gentleman?"

"Oh, she'd seen Clem around a few times, and he's got a hankering for her. Everybody knows that. Guess he knew she'd show up at the Spa—it's the only place open this late."

"Well, what's this about a spoon?" I asked.

"Mean you never heard of the Hermit's Junemoon Spoon? It was given him by his daddy, and *he* got it from *his* daddy—and they was all black ones in the heart. Anybody got hold of that spoon, they ain't no girl can resist him. Hermit used to rent it out, but it caused a lot of trouble so he figured to keep it to hisself."

"Just a minute. Do you mean that that big fellow made time with the lady just because he had that dirty old spoon?"

"Well, son, you seen Clem yourself. Did he look like the kind of feller any girl'd go for? And you seen the look in Julie's eyes. Yessir, she's a goner."

Well, Bernie, it sounded crazy to me—but that babe was too beautiful to forget about. Now, I don't take any stock in charms —they're for suckers. I know, I used to sell them—but there had to be *something* on that guy's side.

I decided to talk more to the old buzzard.

"Sir, do you think this Clem has met success *only* because of that spoon?"

The geezer just laughed.

"Well, boy, you don't need to give up hope. If Clem could talk the Hermit out of it, a good salesman like you probably could too. Clem'll have to bring it back tomorrow morning—it can't ever go out for more than one night. If you're interested, I can tell you where the Hermit lives."

I was about to say nix, but then I remembered about the girl. The way that blue dress creeped around her and how those blonde curls fell over her shoulders. I used my head and tried to look indifferent.

"Of course, I am staying for a few days here," I said, "and a little female company certainly wouldn't do any harm. Naturally, I can't quite believe this 'Junemoon Spoon' story—but if you could give me the young lady's address . . . ?"

"That wouldn't do any good, boy. Julie hates all men, normally, ever since her husband run off. You'll have to get the spoon, if you want to make time. And Julie comes in here for a glass of milk almost every night."

Well, we sat there for a while, and then the old guy got up to leave. I couldn't let this slip through my fingers, so—I don't know exactly why—I asked him for this Hermit bird's address.

"Go down Shell Road till you hit the Bear turn-off. Up about three, four miles is a little cabin. That's where the Hermit lives. You can't miss it, son."

I said thank you. He got up, pulled out the bottle of junk I'd sold him, and said, "Boy, maybe I get this medicine on me, I'll feel like taking on Julie myself, eh?"

I told him sure and he went out, cackling and rubbing the stuff on his face. After a while I walked back to the hotel and spent the night dreaming of this babe.

Words fail me, Bernie. There just aren't any bundles as cute as that, anywheres!

The next day I covered the joint, but thoroughly. When I was finished, there wasn't a drugstore or cafe that didn't stock my pills and jellies. Even wised a gas station to it, and the guy there took the last of the bottles. In two weeks, Bernie, I'd picked up a cool grand. And that's good, even for Harry Jackson, *and* considering the merchandise I had to unload.

But, somehow, my heart wasn't in it. Like I said, I been around—but this tomato, well, she was something more than special. I couldn't shake her out of my head and believe me, I tried hard. But what the heck, business was over and I figured pleasure could begin.

So, after classing up at the hotel, I took Bessie up a couple of dirt roads, past Blacktown and wide stretches of nothing, till I came to a lot of woods and stuff. I hoofed it on from there till I came to an old shack out of *Tobacco Road*.

The door was opened by a bunch of whiskers with a face behind it somewheres. An ancient model, creaking at the axle, waved me to a rickety old stool and said a lot of stuff I couldn't get at first.

You understand, I was taking all this as a joke. I thought maybe there was some screwy southern tradition that I hadn't heard about—and with that babe straining at the throttle, I'd give anything a try.

I saw her in town that day, with a yellow dress she was poured into. She didn't know Harry Jackson from Adam's grandmother, but you can take it from me, Harry Jackson knew her. I started to think of her and me in Hollywood—she'd knock any two-bit press agent back on his heels.

The antique was spouting "y'all's" a mile a minute, but I finally managed to ask him about that spoon gimmick. He cackled away and dug the thing out of a dirty box on the shelf.

The Hermit said he didn't want to rent it out, but of course, when Harry Jackson turns on the old persuasion, look out! I felt silly doing all this, but the yokel looked real serious and said the "Junemoon Spoon" couldn't fail. Said I'd be squiring this chick without any trouble at all, long as I kept the gimmick close to me and waved it in front of her face every now and then.

Well, I talked to him fast and solid and I finally got him to rent the thing to me for the night. It wasn't easy, but a five spot helped. I knew it was money down the drain, but what the heck, how many times do you live? I kept thinking, too, that when I was through with it, I might be able to push the spoon off onto somebody else for quite a nice wad. To that Clem hick, maybe.

So anyway, I got into Bessie and drove back to the hotel for a little last minute repair work. By the time I got to the Spa it was nine-thirty or so and there was the same bunch gathered. They gummed and jawed and I sat down with a beer. It wasn't easy waiting.

Twenty minutes later, the dish walks in. It's a hot night so she is dressed very cool indeed. A pair of Levi's, rolled up past her knees and a faded old shirt, pulled out and made into one of those midriff things—and as far as I could see, that's all. Harry Jackson didn't breathe too easy.

Well, the ugly customer isn't around anywhere, and she sits over in a corner by herself with a glass of milk. So, slapping a smile on the kisser, I beat it over and introduce myself.

"Excuse me, young lady, my name is Harry Jackson. I'm new to this town and I wonder if you'd mind a little company for a few moments—I hope you won't think it brash of me."

She starts to give me the cold shoulder, when I remember the gimmick. So before she can wave goodbye, I pull the spoon out where nobody but her could see it.

You never saw such a change, Bernie. Right away, the second she lays her eyes on that lousy piece of wood, her whole face lights up and she smiles up at me like Harry Jackson was the only guy alive.

What do I do? I sit down. It's made. She tells me her name, she tells me where she lives, all alone, she—but why go into that, know what I mean?

We go over to her place, she shows me her family album (while I'm waving this stick around like crazy) and things really look rosy. Just then, when the Jackson stock is at its peak and I think things couldn't get better, there's a knock at the door.

Julie—that's the babe's name—rushes over and lets in a scroungy pair of females who say they're relatives and want to chat. So there I am, stuck in a house with the most beautiful girl in the world and I got to talk about somebody's cow and why poor Mrs. Fleabody had to go to a foot specialist. It's killing me, you can bet on that, pal. And the kiss-off is when these biddies say they want to spend the night. Spend the night, can you beat it!

Well, I didn't get sore. After all, I figured, it wasn't Julie's fault. She was willing. And before I left she said she'd meet me the next night at the same place. She wouldn't be home to anybody that night, she said. Anybody, that is, but Harry Jackson.

So, I didn't feel too bad when I left. I had plenty of time. And what's more, I started to think more and more about Hollywood, and what Mattie Glickstein would say to something like this Julie gal. So long peddling; hello swimming pool and easy living. Yeah, Bernie, I didn't feel bad at all . . . then.

I steered Bessie back to the shack the next morning and told the Hermit geezer that I wanted to rent his charm again. I ain't ever been much of a philosopher, and what's more, I never believed in good-luck charms. But the way that thing worked —whether it was a custom or a tradition or what the hell it was —I needed it again.

But the old guy said nix. "One night only, absolutely, that's all," he said. So I spieled and argued myself blue in the face, but he wouldn't budge. Here was a chance to get the swellest looking blonde alive plus a million bucks in Hollywood and a ninety year old hermit was standing in my way. Not for Harry Jackson, I said.

There wasn't any question in my mind. If I could get Julie to Hollywood—and I *could* with that spoon!—I'd be in gravy for good. It'd be perfect. So after we hemmed and hawed for an hour and I saw I couldn't talk him into renting it to me I asked if he'd sell it.

The old hick hesitated, like he wouldn't dream of such a thing. Then, when I turned on the pressure, he mellowed up.

"All right, son," he said. "But it's going to be expensive. Very expensive."

I said I didn't care, thinking he'd slap a twenty or thirty dollar tag on it. Thirty bucks would have made him rich, the way it looked to me.

And you could have knocked me over when he straightens up and says, "Very well. You may purchase the Junemoon Spoon for three thousand dollars."

It floored me, you can bet. But I kept thinking of Julie and that swimming pool and Mattie Glickstein's face, so I started to bargain with him.

Bernie, you never run up against such a customer. I've sold a lot of stuff in my time and bargained for a lot, but this bird wouldn't move. When I would mention half or two thirds, he'd turn away like he wasn't interested at all. So I told him no-dice and walked out, hoping he'd stop me. He didn't. So what could you do? There'd be no tonight, no future—and I meant no future, when I remembered the look in Julie's eyes. Harry Jackson don't go overboard on many things, but this babe's promise was worth the whole three grand to me—even if it was half of what I had in the bank.

I went back and he was waiting. A crazy looking galoot, with his filthy shirt and long white beard, but he's the greatest salesman who ever lived. I hate his guts but you got to respect him.

Ten minutes later he had my check and I had the Junemoon Spoon.

Bernie, I'll cut the rest short, because I don't like to think about it. It shows what a filthy, dishonest, lousy life this is and I don't want to turn you against humanity.

By the time I got back to the hotel I was on top of the world. I had figured out just where I'd take Julie—Paramount first—when we'd leave, everything. I thought I'd ask her someday, after we were married, what the story was on this Junemoon Spoon pitch. I figured it was an old Southern custom, handed down from way back.

Anyway, I got to the Spa by nine o'clock, feeling wonderful. I was out three G's, but what was that to what I was getting? Peanuts. I was in for the California gravy. I got a beer and sat down to wait. I held the wooden spoon in my hands, looking at it.

It wasn't very unusual. Just an ordinary spoon, with teeth marks all over it.

Then I saw everybody looking at me and sniggering like they'd heard a big joke, and that didn't make me feel too good, but I didn't give it much thought.

After a while, Julie walks in. But is she different! Brand new dress, flowers in her hair—words fail, Bernie. She smiles around the joint, then she sits down with her glass of milk.

Of course, it doesn't take Harry Jackson a long time to get up and ankle over. But I'm just about to her table, when a great big hulking guy steps up, pushes me aside and sits down. He starts jawing like I wasn't around.

"Oh, Julie," I said, "it's Harry. You haven't forgotten our date, have you?"

She looks at me like death. And when that happens an ice chill goes right to my toes. The big bruiser looks around and I pretend to be ordering something. Then I grab the Spoon and hold it up where the tomato can see it. I wave it around my head, up and down and sideways. But she doesn't even look up.

Then everybody in the dump starts laughing and before I can think straight a greasy mauler comes up and grabs me by the pants and the next thing I know I'm sitting on the ground outside. I hear the place rocking with goofy laughter.

Harry Jackson isn't slow, Bernie. He wasn't born day before yesterday. I took five seconds to get to Bessie and in just a little more time I'm knocking on the Hermit's shack.

"Come on, you dirty, cheap, swindling piker!" I call, but no one answers. I knock so hard the door flies open and I'm staring at an empty room. Empty like nobody had been in it for years.

So I race all over town looking for the crook. But no one knows anything about it. Nobody ever heard of any hermit, like I was crazy in the head or something.

And, Bernie, I'm just about to the point where I figure I *am* soft upstairs. I combed that town but good, but it was no use. Then, after I got tired and disgusted, I went back to my hotel. I saw Julie, that gorgeous, no good dish, walking arm in arm with the bruiser and it broke my heart.

I took that lousy spoon and threw it as far as I could. But that wasn't all, not by a long shot. When I got back to the hotel room, I found it piled high with all that junk I'd peddled. All those stinking bottles, every one that I unloaded in Sneadville, were heaped on the floor.

Not much else to it, Bernie. It was a dirty, crooked trick to play on me but somehow that ain't what bothers me so much. I keep thinking of that beautiful hunk of merchandise. I keep remembering how her hair fit around her shoulders and how the sides of her mouth crinkled up when she smiled. Can you imagine Harry Jackson out three G's and he thinks about a dame?

No justice in this world, I tell you. None.

Time and Again

His manner was courteous and, I thought, a little sad at the task before him—which was to cheat me. He glanced away from the books nervously. "Of course, you understand, Mr. Friedman," he said, "there's practically no call whatever for this sort of thing these days."

I nodded. He was a bright lad: the meaning of my smile did not go by him. He averted his eyes. I think it was this gesture —of sweeping the eyes downward, of profound embarrassment —that first set me to wondering where our paths might have crossed before.

"The universities aren't buying much any more; that could have been an outlet. Can't even sell them folklore, though. Which makes it rough, you see." He drew a deep breath. "To tell you the truth, sir, we actually couldn't use your library at all and, frankly, I'd be taking a big chance to make you any kind of an offer." The words came out hyphenated: an unhappy schoolboy's mumbling fulfillment of the week's elocution assignment. His ears were burning.

"However," he went on, "since-I'm-here-I'll-take-the-risk-just-to-get-them-off-your-hands." He had unconsciously withdrawn a pristine copy of Breasted's excellent study; his fingers ran along the finely tooled leather. It was an example of Bayntun's best work.

"That is very kind of you," I said, "under the circumstances."

He blushed. It was amusing, how carelessly he replaced the book, suddenly conscious of the tactical error. He took a checkbook from his pocket. "Five—" His voice quavered a moment and then switched to a defensively arrogant authoritativeness. "Five hundred dollars is the limit we could possibly go," he said, still looking at the rug.

I felt sorry for the boy. Quite apart from the growing sense of recognition, he was plainly intelligent and agonized at the ignominy of his position. He had been unable to conceal his excitement at my library—I'd collected for many years and in many lands and the collection abounded with choice items. Many volumes had cost considerably in excess of the price I was now being offered for the lot. And the boy knew it. Clearly.

"Very well," I said, perhaps maliciously, "if you think that a fair bid, I accept."

He swallowed. Then he unscrewed his pen and began to fill in the check. He got no further than the date. "Mr. Friedman," he said, slowly, "on second thought, the risk is too great. I'm—afraid I'll have to withdraw the offer. We can't use these books."

"Oh? Pity. I'd hoped you could—you see, I'm leaving for Cairo next week. Probably for good. Well, no harm done; there are other book stores, now, aren't there. What about Martindale's? Do you suppose they might—"

"Sir—" The boy tore up the check and walked over to my bookcases. He looked up suddenly: the feeling of familiarity burst powerfully at this exact instant: somewhere, at some time, I'd seen that face. But not merely the face. More disturbing, the entire personality was closely associated with my memory.

"Sir, I've got to tell you something."

"By all means."

He licked his lips and dropped his eyes to the folio of pre-Dynastian tablets he'd removed. "This library," he said, "is worth a great deal of money. It's by far the finest collection of Egyptology I've ever seen. To give you a fair price, I'd have to write you out a check for five thousand dollars, not five hundred. Even at that, we could turn a nice profit."

"But," I said, "if they're not in demand . . ."

"I lied, Mr. Friedman. That's my job: to lie. Had you really accepted the store's offer—I'm only authorized to write checks up to five hundred dollars; I went my limit—we would have made close to a thousand per cent profit."

I put a look of surprise on my face, though of course I was not in the least surprised. "Why are you telling me this?" I asked.

He shrugged. "Maybe because I'm a lousy businessman. I

don't know; it doesn't matter. You could do me a favor though
and not mention this to anybody."

"Sit down, won't you?" I said. "Surely the chief buyer for the
town's largest bookstore has the authority to waste a little time
—if not money."

He slumped into the chair and folded his hands. Thin, pale
hands. Artist's hands. Almost to himself, he said, "There are at
least three universities I know of that would have gone crazy
trying to outbid each other over your set. High bids."

"You *are* a lousy businessman," I smiled. "Picking up the
Breasted was fatal, you know."

"I know. Look—why don't you take them with you, or dis-
pose of them privately, or even give them away. But don't call a
bookstore. You'll only get cheated. Believe me. They're—we're
—like used car dealers, except used car dealers have more love
for their merchandise. More understanding, anyway."

"You love books very much, don't you?" I said.

He seemed glad to admit it, or glad not to have to be ashamed
to admit it. "Yes; I'm afraid I do."

"That's a pretty serious affliction, for a buyer. Tell me, why do
you do it?" I did not think myself capable of such a tactless question. But it was too late.

He smiled. "Well, it's this habit I've picked up. Eating."

I felt the bitterness of his voice unlock other doors of
memory. The conjunction of this room was part of it, too. Part
of the secret of where I had seen the boy before. It had, I was
confident, been in this very library. And yet, he'd not been here
ever before. I *had* to know.

"What is your name?" I asked, somewhat abruptly.

"Hoffman," he said. "Maurice Hoffman."

It didn't help. The name meant nothing to me. We shook
hands; and at the touch, the sadness of Maurice Hoffman trans-
mitted itself to me, and another door came open. It had been
long ago—that's for certain. Very long ago. I mixed some high-
balls.

"The usual first novel?" I said, hoping to cheer him, hoping
to learn more.

He crumpled an empty cigarette package and took one of mine. "Four novels," he said. "Over a hundred short stories."

"Rejected?"

He nodded.

I fumbled. "Were they good?"

"No," he said, with finality. "No. You see, Mr. Friedman, the thing is: just because you love books and literature, that doesn't have a damn thing to do with whether or not you're a good writer."

"Well, but isn't that what accounts for the great number of practicing critics?" The joke was bad. My visitor was old, very old; I saw that good-humored commiseration would only sound foolish. He had tried and he had failed. It showed in his eyes.

I was immediately, and a bit unreasonably, overcome with concern. And still another door creaked open. Writer. Unsuccessful writer. With sad eyes.

"Perhaps," I said, "that's why I chose my own special field. Egyptology doesn't present much in the way of competition."

"That isn't what's wrong. I'm just not any good, that's all. My work," he said definitely, "smells."

"I'm sorry." I thought of how it might have affected me to have failed in my profession and been forced to content myself with sweeping out the Cairo museum after hours.

He drank most of the highball at a swallow. "No—I'm the one to be sorry," he said. "I've taken up a lot of your time. Well, it doesn't happen very often, thank God. I'm actually quite happy. Really I am. I'll open a store of my own some day; nothing pretentious: but the kind you see on sidestreets, you know: Ye Old Rare Book Shoppe, that sort of thing. Where the kindly old proprietor sits perched on a ladder and makes you buy a copy of Strindberg's *Spook Sonata* and if you don't have enough money, well, pay for it when you can. I won't get rich. But it's better than working in a freight company or a sawmill and at least I won't have to cheat people like you." He rose and extended his hand. "Goodbye, Mr. Friedman. Please—for me: don't sell them. They're scholarly, beautiful things and you've loved them for a long time. I know you have. To a bookstore they'll be so much merchandise, to the libraries they'll be relics; believe me, they'll gather dust and rot. Treat them right. Because—well, because there aren't many important things left in the world. But these—" he looked at the books and ran his hands delicately, lovingly along the spines "—these are important."

I felt suddenly very young and stupid. I wanted to thank the lad, for I had been about to sell what had once been—and was now!—a part of my soul; and he had stopped me. "Where are you going now?" I asked, unsure of what I meant.

"Back to the store," he said. "Then, I don't know, home; why? Sleep. Then maybe on the weekend I'll take a swim. There's a reservoir up in the hills where I live—not many people know about it. You can swim there at night if you want to, the water's pretty clean, considering. I like to swim. Mr. Friedman—don't, look, don't worry about me. I'm going to be all right. Just some adjusting to do."

He pressed my hand and the door closed and he was gone. I tried to forget the look on his face.

But I could not forget.

The final packing and arrangements for my passage consumed much time, but even so I found it impossible to be rid of the question: *Where had I seen Maurice Hoffman before?*

It remained in my mind, annoying by day and tortuous by night, throughout the trip, which was a long one. Finally it was over: a great deal of work awaited me in Cairo and in time I forgot about the boy.

It was at the conclusion of a field trip that the image was unexpectedly brought up again—and the riddle, at least the immediate one, solved.

I had been going through some of my books, the few it had seemed prudent to take along, searching for data concerning the site of the village of El Amarna. Lovett's *Wonders of the Nile* was proving inadequate to my needs; it was a superior work aesthetically, but it bristled with romantic, and highly unscientific, speculation. I required specific information and was about to lay the book aside when the splendidly printed illustrations caught my attention.

It was Plate VI that made my heart tighten. This photograph depicted the mummy of a young man, with a subplate below of the casket bearing his meticulously rendered likeness. The caption read:

> HUYA-SON-OF-TERURA. Born 1362 B.C. Tomb uncovered by Prof. Richard von Hanstein's fruitful expedition of 1926 into the Sakkarah site region. The casket was found to contain numerous documents and tablets revealing this man's occupation to be that of an artist. Translation of a document bearing the seal of Akhnaton I discloses Huya-son-of-Terura elected to take his own life. The body was perfectly preserved and a member of the expedition, Dr. Carl Baumgartner, states that drowning was the probable cause of death . . .

The resemblance was almost unbelievable. It could easily have been a photograph of Maurice Hoffman in fourteenth century B.C. habit: the sadness of the eyes, the placid acceptance of defeat, the features down to the last minute detail, everything —more than a likeness. They were identical.

It often requires many hours for a human to rationalize his own inmost fears into logical skepticism. Before I could manage to persuade myself that it was a coincidence and nothing more, I had a cable addressed to the bookstore in California; a cable begging for information concerning Maurice Hoffman, clerk, Jewish-American.

The answering letter, from the bookkeeper, arrived several weeks later by regular mail. It was brief and businesslike:

> Dear Mr. Friedman:
> In response to your cable, we regret to inform you that our former employee, Maurice Hoffman, died under tragic circumstances two-and-one-half months ago.

His body was found in a reservoir near his home. An autopsy revealed that he had drowned, and, as he had been known to swim in this reservoir on certain evenings, it was generally agreed that he must have suffered an attack of cramps.

If you wish further information, I would suggest that you contact Maurice's mother, Rhoda Hoffman . . .

I tore the letter and the book plate into hundreds of small pieces and threw the pieces into the hot desert wind.

They are lost now, covered over with centuries. But I cannot forget. Sometimes, when the moon is clear upon the sand, I think of the two unhappy young men, and I feel that I am an animal which has wandered too far from the clear safety of its home.

A very old animal, and afraid.

A Friend of the Family

She was talking about what a wonderful show, what wonderful dancers, what wonderful hands on that woman in the organdy dress, and while she was talking, he was thinking: Miss Kelly, you're a very pretty girl. He decided to hold her closer. It worked fine. They swayed smoothly to the off-tempo rhythms of the four old men who were playing *Basin Street* half sad, half happy, all wrong.

"Are you having any fun?" Reynolds asked. He had to be sure.

"Yes," the girl said, and pressed her body closer to his. "I'm having a wonderful time." Her eyes were shut.

Always before, he thought, she'd answered, "Yes, Mr. Reynolds, I'm having a very good time, thank you very much." Now it was *wonderful*—without the Mr. Reynolds. And he liked it. He liked her, too, as she was now, tonight: Ruth. Not Miss Kelly.

Who was Miss Kelly?

A cornet strained for a high note, didn't make it, bleated painfully. Someone said, "Ouch!" The music trailed off, instrument by instrument, and the musicians sat down and wiped their faces. It was hot. Smoky and hot.

"Let's get a drink," Reynolds said. "You want to?"

"Sure," the girl said.

They pardoned and elbowed their way back to the little circular table. He walked behind her and kept thinking about what a pretty girl she was and what was wrong with him that he hadn't noticed this in all these years.

She slid into her chair and pretended to fan herself with a bar menu.

"Same?" he said.

"No," she said. "I think I'll try something new."

"Be careful."

"Why?" She laughed and adjusted the straps of her evening

118

gown. It was cut low. Her chest was dotted with little brown freckles. "It's all right to mix," she said. "It won't hurt you."

"That a fact?"

"Yup." She looked terribly young in this light, much younger than she actually was. "It's all according to how fast you drink, not *what*. I mean about the system absorbing too much alcohol too fast for the brain. That's what makes you woozy."

"Oh. I see." One of her pet words. Woozy—for drunk. Simple-minded, but, somehow, cute. A little like Janet, back before she'd gotten sick: always going around calling everybody ridiculous names ...

Reynolds shook his head. Don't start it, he thought. For God's sake, now, don't start it.

"Yes, sir?" A shapely girl in a barmaid's uniform appeared out of the smoke-haze.

"Another on-the-rocks for me. And—"

"I'll take a Silver Fizz," Ruth said.

"What in the name of digestion is a Silver Fizz?"

"Who knows?"

The orchestra began to play again. A rumba. It made Reynolds feel good: he listened to the noise and watched the people getting up to dance.

"Chug-a-lug?" Ruth said, wrinkling her nose at him. He grinned and they threw down their drinks.

"I intend," Reynolds said, feeling dizzy, "to ask you a question."

"Oh-oh. That sounds grim."

"Very grim, indeed. Miss K: you've been enjoying yourself?"

"Lord, yes," she said. "I've told you that eighteen times already."

He watched her face carefully. "Let's make it for tomorrow then."

It almost happened, the thing he feared, the drawing up; but it didn't. Ruth smiled. "You mean tomorrow?"

"And the day after that," he said, "and the day after that. What do you say?"

He thought about the evening, the first in—how long?—that

he'd had a good time, honestly, without faking, without saying, Forgive me, Janet, forgive me, I'm sorry. It hadn't gone right the first few times. Stiff, formal, strained; boss-secretary relationship: "Good night, Mr. Reynolds" and "Good night, Miss Kelly." She hadn't done much talking then. Even tonight, right through dinner, she was quiet, reserved. But afterwards—something had happened, he knew it. He didn't know what. At the ballet, and then at the Tropics; and now . . .

"Please, Ruth," he said. "It would mean a lot to me."

But she wasn't Ruth any more. She was Miss Kelly sitting there, and he felt embarrassed and ashamed, caught out. She was looking at him and thinking, he could see that, thinking very hard.

Then she said, "All right, if you really want to," and the smile was back and Ruth was back. "But you better promise not to scream at me when I mess up your dictation."

"I promise," he said, and touched her hand.

And thought, so it does end. Janet had been right. For almost a year you fall, and you keep falling, and you almost hit bottom —and then you meet a Ruth. And the awful sore spots begin to hurt a little less.

He wanted to talk to this girl, to tell her what she had done, let her know, somehow, if he could, what this night was meaning to him.

"It was something with gin."

He stopped thinking. "What was?"

"The Silver Fizz. I tasted gin."

Now he found that he wanted to kiss her. Wanted badly, very much to kiss her. "Ruth," he said, "let's get out of here. I'd like—"

"Well, Wally Reynolds, for God's sakes, you old horse thief!"

The voice was strident and booming. Reynolds looked around to face a thin yellowish man with a long pitted nose and a little brush of mustache. The man was grinning widely.

"Hello, Pearson. Ruth, this is our claims agent, Mr.—"

"I know Mr. Pearson," Ruth said. "Hello."

"Hiya." The man wobbled slightly, but his speech was clear. "Got company?"

"Tell you the truth, Eddie," Reynolds said, "we were just getting ready to leave. Kind of late. Got to rise and shine tomorrow, you know."

"Sure," Pearson said. "Sure. But you can have one more, can't you? One more tiny one, for Auld Lang Syne?" He didn't wait for an answer. He pulled a chair from one of the other tables and winked at the waitress. She came over.

"Folksies?" Pearson said.

Reynolds sighed and sank back in the seat. "Bourbon with seven," he said. "Ruth?"

"The same, I guess."

"Make it three," Pearson said, chuckling. "Yes, sir, three little old bombshells." He waved the girl away. "Well, Wally, doggone it, how the devil are you, anyway?"

"I'm all right, Eddie. Yourself?"

"You know me—if I was any healthier, they'd shoot me." Pearson slapped the table and squinted at Ruth. "Looking mighty fancy tonight, Miss Kelly, if you don't mind a man saying so."

Ruth said, "Thank you," and looked over quickly at Reynolds. Her smile was perfunctory.

"Mighty fancy, yes, indeedy." Pearson laughed wetly, shook his head. "That Wally, I tell *you*. Always could pick them. But now you take me—have I got a pretty gal along this evening? Nope I do not, no sir. Stagging it. Always alone, stagging it, that's Eddie. Isn't that right, Wally?"

"That's right," Reynolds said. He wanted desperately to get out. The glow of the evening had been so perfect, it had all been so perfect. He didn't want anything to spoil it. And, all at once, he was afraid.

The drinks came. Eddie Pearson reached into his pocket and drew out a five dollar bill and laid it on the platter. "Keep the change," he said to the waitress. Then, leaning forward, he raised his glass. "Come on, now," he said, "let's do it. Over the lips and past the gums, watch out, stomach, here it comes!"

Reynolds closed his eyes.

Pearson leaned back, ran his tongue along his mustache, bit off the end of a small cigar. "Well," he said, "you're all right,

Wally, you're okay." He jerked a thumb at Reynolds. "Good man, Miss Kelly."

Ruth smiled formally. A quick smile.

"Aye, got to hand it to the old mule-skinner."

"Eddie," Reynolds said, "if you don't mind, it's getting—"

"I mean," Pearson pressed on, "I think it's the greatest thing in the world. I swear to God I do."

"What's the greatest thing in the world?" Reynolds asked, feeling his throat tighten.

"What you're doing, boy. What you're doing! The way you've held up—it's wonderful. By golly, I admire that in a man. Don't you admire that in a man, Miss Kelly?"

"I certainly do, Mr. Pearson," Ruth said.

"Yes, indeedy. But now, you take me for instance. Think I'd have that kind of guts? Heck *no*, I wouldn't. I only been married half as long as old Wally here was, but if anything was to happen to Liz—well, you know me. First thing right off the bat I'd lose my grip, break all up, end of the world. You know what I mean? Seriously." Pearson gulped his drink. "Like when we were having Eddie Junior—Wally can tell you—God, I fussed and fumed and bellered around like an idiot. For why? Because I was scared green about what might happen to the old lady. A simple thing like having a baby, and it set me off. And if she had kicked the bucket, believe me, I'd of just wizened up and died, like the fella says. But—" he shrugged, "—at least I've got sense enough to know it's stupid. So I mean it when I say I'd give my right arm for Wally's guts."

Reynolds was silent. He watched Pearson, studied the man's face, and felt a burning in his heart. Why had he and Janet ever let this blabbermouth into their house, anyway? Why? Sure, he's loaded. But he knows what he's doing. And I know what he's doing. And it doesn't help.

"Man's got to be big," Pearson was saying. "Me? I'm plain old not a big man. I know, I know—Liz tells me the same things Janet used to tell you, Wally. We get into those conversations once in a while; you'd be surprised. I mean, you know: 'If I go first, dear, you've got to promise to go on. Your life can't just stop . . .' And that kind of stuff. Didn't Janet say those identical same words to you?"

"Yes," Reynolds said.

"There you are. She *meant* them, too. Doggone, but you had you a good woman, Wally. A real lady. But, I mean, Liz is the same way. 'Well,' I say, 'Oh, sure, honey, don't you worry, little Eddie'll make out okay. In fact, I'll probably go straight from the funeral and find me some classy broad—' You know, kidding her along, making a joke out of it. But, brother! Just between you and me and the gate post, if it ever did happen, I'd not be around very long afterwards. She might just as well move on over . . ."

Ruth stared at her drink, silently.

Pearson laughed again and thumped the table. "No guts," he said. "It's nothing but weakness with a capital weak. And that's the way human beings are." He made an ice cube bob with his finger. "I don't give a darn what they say, boy, you're acting the way a man ought to, in my book. The sensible way. You're picking up the pieces. You're—"

"What do they say, Eddie?" Reynolds asked.

"Who?" Pearson looked confused. Then, "Oh—you know. What's the diff? You're above that kind of thing."

"What do they say?"

"The usual guff, Wally, just what you'd expect. 'Only one year' and 'Not even a year and already he's stepping high' and like that. Dopes. Like Liz—I mean, I ain't trying to make her any better than she is. She's got her faults, the good Lord knows. Liz don't understand. Unless a man mopes around and bawls like a baby, she figures nothing means anything to him. He don't really care."

Reynolds' fists were clenched now. "But—you tell her different, don't you, Eddie?"

"You betcha my boots I do, pal. And how. As a matter of fact—" Pearson looked over his shoulder, bent forward ". . . we got into a beaut only last week. She'd heard, you know, that you and Miss Kelly here was seeing a little of each other—now don't ask me how she knew! By Harry, you know women: noses in *every*body's business. Anyway, she made sort of a criticism, you see. Snotty remark. I rared back and said, 'Look! Why don't you make up your mind how you think a man ought to act? It just so happens *I'm* a good friend of Wally Reynolds' and I don't give a hoot and a holler what you *think* you know. I can guarantee you of one thing—' Really give it to her, see what I mean? I says, 'I never knew of any two people happier in my life than Janet and Wally Reynolds. And I never saw anybody who could've felt worse at his wife's death. And you open your big yap about Wally again and I'll let you have it!'" Pearson scowled and pulled at his drink. "They don't understand," he said.

Ruth took a cigarette case from her purse. Her cheeks were red. Reynolds looked at her and she looked back, helplessly.

"Just don't understand," Pearson stated. "Whole damn lot of them—excuse the language, Miss Kelly, but it makes me mad. Wally, what's the matter with people? The boss, for instance. Now you'd think a man like O. D. would be able to tell the difference, wouldn't you?"

"What did O. D. say?"

"I hate to tell you. 'Well, well,' he says to me in the hall one day, 'Wallace seems to have made a quick recovery!' Yeah. See what I mean, though? By him you're a callous, hard-hearted—I don't know what. You never was in love with Janet. Her dying of a disease didn't faze you, didn't mean nothing in the whole wide world to you—*all* because you didn't stay broken up, because you're trying to salvage something out of life, you know?" He looked at Ruth. "All because you're trying to pick up the pieces."

Reynolds drained his glass.

"Well, you know what Eddie Pearson says? Eddie Pearson says more power to you, boy. If a man can do it, by the Lord, more power to him! Right, Miss Kelly?"

Ruth's eyes were moist. She did not answer. Reynolds got up, his legs trembling. "Thanks for the drink, Eddie," he said. "Thanks for everything."

Pearson stuck out his hand. "Guess I'll stag it for a while. Old lady'll kill me one way or the other. What the heck, I don't know, maybe you're not so bad off at that, in a way, huh, Wally?" He winked. "I ain't forgot *my* batchin' days. Won't have one more real short one, will you? One little one?"

Reynolds pulled his hand away and helped Ruth with her jacket.

He did not say goodbye to Pearson.

Outside of the crowded room, outside in the cool night air, he drew reality into his mind. He opened one door and waited, got in the other side.

He drove from the lot out onto the wide dark sweep of highway that ran close to the ocean.

After a long while the girl next to him said, "I'm sorry."

"It's all right, Miss Kelly," he said, lighting a cigarette slowly and pulling the smoke deep into his lungs. "It isn't your fault."

It isn't anybody's fault, he thought. Pearson was a malicious, blundering fool—but he would have found out anyway. Or perhaps he'd known all along. And could he blame them, really?

He and Janet had loved one another, and they'd been happy, and it had been right. And can that happen twice in a man's life?

He drove in silence, his mind webbed in memories, to the large tan-brick apartment unit; turned the key, started out of the car.

"Wait."

He glanced over at the girl and saw, for the first time, that she had been crying. Her face was streaked, and in the soft amber lights she looked more lovely than ever. But there was something else there now. Something new. In her eyes.

"Are you going to take me out tomorrow night?" she asked, in a hushed voice. "And the night after that, and the night after that?" She moved close to him. "It would mean a lot to me."

He thought of Janet and of the words she had said to him, of a thousand perfect hours.

"Why would it mean a lot to you?" he asked.

The girl touched his hand, and he felt the warmth of her. He saw the pleading in her eyes.

"Perhaps you're not the only one who is lonely," she said, softly. "Perhaps you're not the only one who has lost something."

He looked at her for a very long time, trying to understand; to believe. Then, suddenly, he took her into his arms and kissed her. And with her lips upon his, he knew that he was safe, now, from all the Pearsons in the world. He was safe from the Pearsons in his mind.

A heavy, dark weight seemed to slip away and vanish.

"You know something, Miss Kelly?" he said. "I think I love you."

And he thought: Janet would have loved you, too.

Mr. Underhill

Why, I was their oldest employee! I really was, and that thought never occurred to me until just now. I knew I'd been with the company quite a little while, but—twenty-seven years! Three-months-and-fourteen-days!

That's what makes it harder than ever to understand. It isn't, after all, that I wasn't doing the work; and a body knows it couldn't have been my joke that was responsible.

Something tells me it must have started when Soapy Levinson put the octopus in the water-cooler.

Of course, it wasn't a real octopus—only one of those play rubber things you get in the dime store—but it sure stirred up a riot. That was the way with Soapy: He's a very comical fellow, been with the firm only six years and already he's a dispatcher, so you can see it wasn't all shenanigans with him. But how those girls did laugh! They laughed until I was afraid they'd take the convulsions, especially Mrs. Fredrickson (she posts). And I'll never forget how funny it was when he came into the office one day all stooped over like a midget, you see, and said to Maggie the switchboard operator: "I want to see the Big Man here!"

I'm not very funny, myself. Didn't feel it was right to waste time with jokes when I was young, and then when I wasn't young anymore there didn't seem much point.

There was a time, though, when they all used to try to get me into their games and silly things like that, but I always frowned and pretended I was working. Pretty soon they stopped asking me, and I didn't like that very much, either. And with the new crowd it got so finally they wouldn't talk to me at all, except Mr. Norgesand and every once in a while he'd stop by the desk and say, "Well, how's the old machine tickin' today?" He didn't mean anything wrong in that, but somehow it made me feel peculiar.

That's what happened right after the joke about the octopus

that Soapy pulled. Mr. Norgesand saying that about the machine ticking, I mean.

And it must have started me off thinking a little.

Now, I was what they call a Tracer, with the company. Naturally, I started out as an errand boy, but I gradually moved up and I imagine I did a pretty fair job, otherwise why would Mr. Nims say, and then Mr. Norgesand after him, that they didn't think it would be right to move me up to anything else? They always said that I was one Tracer out of a million, which is a very nice thing for an employer to say.

That's why I always tried to do a good job, because of the faith they had in me. Plus the fact that I never did get excited when customers would call up shouting about what happened to their shipments and what was wrong with our company anyway? I was always very courteous and only once did I ever shout back, and then nobody heard me and it was never reported so I imagine one slip didn't work against me.

Well, about this time everybody in the office had all gone back to work and things were going right along schedule. Soapy and Mr. Norgesand and a few others were out to the coffee wagon downstairs, so it was quiet and peaceful, no one to bother me. I wasn't thinking about anything in particular, I don't think, so I didn't know why I jumped when the teletype started buzzing.

The message was from San Francisco, from one of the girls there. It said: EMPIRE LAUNDRY SHORT THREE CTNS NBN I/S FTTGS. MUST HAVE IMMEDIATE REPLY.

And it was right then I got the idea of the joke, right at that minute! At first I was afraid to, but there wasn't anybody watching, so I sent back: TELL THEM TO GET ANOTHER COMPANY IF THEY'RE SO FUSSY. MEANTIME WILL SEE WHAT CAN BE DONE.

From out of the blue sky I thought of a name and signed it: GEORGE W. UNDERHILL.

You see! I made it up out of my head, and I wish I could have seen that girl's face in San Francisco when she got it. It was the same girl who'd been sending messages to me for seven years!

Later on, of course, I got the matter of the short straightened out. But even then I signed it UNDERHILL, only without the George W. on.

Well sir, I didn't tell anybody about this until I'd done it two or three more times. The operators in the other stations just guessed it was some new man taken over my old job, though none of them ever asked what had happened to me, which hurt, kind of.

Finally I couldn't hold it in, because I knew it was a really good joke that everybody would appreciate, counting Mr. Norgesand, who always laughed at Soapy Levinson. The first one I told was Joe Fadness (claims), asking him to keep it a secret, but I knew he wouldn't.

I didn't know what to think when Joe didn't laugh. He just looked at me and said, "What's the point, Mac?" And that spoiled the fun a little.

"No point, Joe," I said, chuckling. "It was a joke."

He looked at me. "A joke, huh? Mean you wrote out this here message and signed somebody else's name to it?"

"That's what I did, Joe."

He smiled and right then I saw he caught on. "Well now, Mac," he said, "that's a real funny one, you bet, a real funny one."

I waited for him to stop laughing, then I went back to work.

But for some reason I couldn't understand, Joe didn't spread the word about my joke. Maybe it was because he thought I was spoofing him, and a serious person like myself wouldn't do a kid's trick.

But I got ashamed of myself after a while for keeping it all in and not telling everybody. The reason I didn't before was I was afraid to, in a way, because then they might think I was another regular cut-up like Soapy and be at me all the time to join in their games, which didn't really fit an older man. I was afraid of losing their respect.

Well, I was working away when Bakersfield teletyped down asking for a report on an overage, and I couldn't resist one more time. Thought of the way one of those cocky young solicitors would do it, and sent: ARE THEY SUCH A BIG COMPANY

THEY CAN'T USE A LITTLE EXTRA FREE MERCHAN-
DISE? Signed: UNDERHILL.

And I like to died because Sophie the stenographer got ahold
of the strip from the waste basket. The look on her face! First
she stared at the strip, then at me (no one had used the teletype
since), then back at the strip. Then she scratched her head and
took it over to Bill Stoddard, and they talked about it.

Bill came over in a little while, grinning. "Hey, Mac," he said,
sitting down on my desk, "you do this?"

I frowned and looked at him through my eye-shade.

"Do what, Bill?" I winked at Joe, who had stopped his work.

"This business about Underhill? That your doing?"

"Well . . . to tell the truth . . ." I suppose I blushed, and snapped
my black arm-guards. Bill didn't do anything for a minute but
stare at me, then all of a sudden he started to laugh, and I declare
that boy laughed so hard I was sure he'd hurt his stomach!

Made me feel good, you know! Don't see why, but it did,
because in a minute Bill had told Sophie and Sophie had told
Maggie and pretty soon Mrs. Fredrickson and all the rest were,
well, they were almost crying!

Naturally, Mr. Norgesand came out to see what all the fuss
was about.

"Settle down now," he said in a loud voice. "Soapy, what've
you been up to this time?"

But Soapy was laughing, too. He started to speak up, but then
he turned red and he could only point at me. By this time I was
wishing they'd stop it.

"Mac, what in the world—"

"Really, Mr. Norgesand," I tried to say, "it was only a little
practical joke." I explained it to him. But somehow it didn't
strike Mr. Norgesand funny: He looked at the rest and said
something very peculiar. He said, "You ought to be ashamed,
the bunch of you!" Then he went back in his office, but I could
see from the corner of my eye that he only waited to be by himself to laugh too.

Oh, let me tell you, it went over big, all right.

They all started to call me Mr. Underhill after that. And it really got to be the office joke, as Joe or Maggie or whoever it happened to be, would do things like get calls and say: "I'm sorry, but I'll have to turn you over to our Mr. Underhill. I'm sure he'll be able to help you." Then I'd be stuck with whoever it was, and there were some mighty embarrassing moments.

In a while I was sorry I'd started it at all, they ran it in the ground so. Every other call was for Mr. Underhill. "The most efficient, best-looking, go-getter in the business," Bill Stoddard would say and then give me the call. It got to be awful and I dreaded it.

Once somebody called and asked Joe who was in charge of tracing.

"Our Mr. Underhill," he said. "Best man on any tracing desk in the country."

"New, isn't he?" they asked.

"Only to this office. Been in the game a while, but that isn't the point. That guy's going up like a rocket. Another ten years he'll have Norgesand's job, between you and me. Never makes a mistake, always on time, always courteous! How could he lose?"

Now that was the silliest thing I'd ever heard. I never made mistakes, myself, I was always courteous and on time and everything Joe said. Yet it sounded hard to put together. He was describing me, in a way, then again he certainly wasn't. I felt that something was missing, because I knew as well as my life they'd never put me anywhere else. After I heard Joe say these things, I couldn't concentrate all day until quitting time.

It was about three months afterwards, and they wouldn't still let go of the joke, even though they must have been able to see how sick I was of it. I even remember it was eleven o'clock in the morning. I'd been having just a little bit of bad luck, somehow, as through no fault of my own—since I was always courteous —some pretty big clients had dropped our company. Couldn't understand this, because I agreed with everything they said and tried to be sympathetic.

Well, it was eleven o'clock, as I said, when I got up and went into the gentleman's lounge, which was my custom at this particular time. When I got back, there was this fellow in Mr. Norgesand's office.

Now a lot of people came to see Mr. Norgesand in the course of the day, so I don't know exactly what it was, but I couldn't seem to be able to take my eyes off of this one. He was around thirty, I'd say, with fat red cheeks and wavy blonde hair, and from his suit handkerchief pocket there were three cigars. Never did care for cigars, but even so this couldn't have been the reason I started not to like that young fellow.

Mr. Norgesand, he rose up and stretched across the desk to shake hands, then after a while they came out and over to my own desk.

"Mac," Mr. Norgesand said, putting his hand on my back, "I want you to meet George. George, this is Mac, who I was telling you about."

I shook his hand.

"Mac, that is, Mr. Kibber, here, has been our Tracer for quite a while, haven't you, Mac?"

I said yes, I had.

"A good worker, a hard worker, but, well, business is booming, George, as I don't have to tell a sharp boy like you! Booming, yes sir, and I'm afraid there's a bit more than old Mac can handle. Mac, George here is going to pitch in and give you a hand. He's a young man, wants to learn the ropes—and I can't think of a better way, can you? Later on we may work him into something, eh Mac?"

I smiled courteously and told Mr. Norgesand that though I didn't really think there was too much for me, I'd be glad to help teach the young man. He, this fellow, hadn't said a word yet. Only smiled with his big teeth, which were all white and even.

When we were alone I had him draw up a chair next to the desk.

"Well," I said, trying to be friendly, "so you're just starting out, are you?"

"Got it wrong, Pops," he said, "dead wrong. This is my line, know what I mean, *my line*, and when something's *your line* you're never just 'starting out'—know what I mean?"

I said yes, but I couldn't make anything out of that, to tell the truth.

He was awfully large, for being so young. He took out one of his cigars and pointed it at me.

"Join me in a bomber?"

He made an ugly round O with his lips and put the cigar inside and lit the cigar with a big silver lighter that must have cost him a lot of money.

"Okay, Dad, don't feel you got to sing me any songs—know this stuff like a book. Like a book. So you just work on and we'll chat like you're teaching me something, okay? That'll keep the old man happy. I can see he digs industry."

When he started doodling funny pictures on the back of an invoice, as I was explaining a complicated procedure, I said, "See here, now, my boy! I'd appreciate your attention, Mr.—"

"Call me George, Pops. Real George—get it? The last name is Underhill."

Don't you know that startled me at first, considering that I had made George W. Underhill up out of my head?

"W.?" I asked.

"Couldn't be righter if you strained."

I started to tell him what a funny coincidence it was, but frankly I didn't think he'd understand the joke. And about that time everybody stopped talking about it anyway—for fear of confusion, no doubt—so I buckled down to give him what I had. He drew pictures all the time I spoke, too.

At first it was awful, because I couldn't understand what the lad was saying whenever he did say anything. Once he reached over and took off my eye-shade and said: "Crazy hat, man!" Another time he looked at my apron, which is leather and protects my trousers from carbon lint and pencil dust, and just said: "Cool." There were lots of other peculiar things he came out with, but I can't remember them.

Which was bad enough, but since it was my understanding that I was to coach young Mr. Underhill, I became angry when he started taking the calls when I'd go to the water cooler or to the gentleman's lounge. Finally it got so bad, his taking liberties like that, that I spoke to Mr. Norgesand about it. Do you know what he said?

"Let the boy alone, Mac. He's doing fine. Found that Siller Pipe short in two seconds—I watched him."

A pure stroke of luck, anyone could see!

But that was only the beginning. On the fourth day since he came, I punched in twenty minutes early, and there he was proud-as-you-please, with his feet propped up on my desk! He was wearing a double-breasted blue suit with a red-white-and-blue striped silk tie and one of those tabbed-collar things, and there was smoke all over. I could hardly talk.

"Little bird with yellow bill, perched upon my windowsill, cocked his shiney eye and said, 'Ain't you 'shamed, you sleepy head?'" was what he told me.

"What is the meaning of this?" I demanded.

"Just workin', Dad, workin'. Got half the morning's stuff cleared away already. Just a second—" He picked up the telephone and dialed outside. "Mr. Hatterman? Underhill. Yes, you can put the stopper on that worry kick—your cartons will be delivered by two o'clock this afternoon. Yes sir."

"Was that Hatterman of Pacific?" I asked.

"Deedy deed."

"But those cartons of his were smashed on the dock yesterday!"

"Don't *worry* about it! Tell him that and he'd blow his stack. He's happy now and I'll think of something later on. Take it easy."

I didn't say a word to him all day, except to tell him to take the chair and give me back my desk. "Sure thing, Boss-Man!" he answered.

That night Mr. Norgesand called me into his office and asked how Mr. Underhill was coming along.

"Well, sir, he may be a hard worker, but his manner on the phone isn't what you'd call courteous, really."

"Lost any business through him?"

"No sir, not yet."

"Gained any?"

"Well ... Merchant Fruit *did* swing over to us, but I think they would have anyway. I've been working on them."

Mr. Norgesand looked at me. He said "Yes" and allowed me to go back. Underhill was at my desk again and I had to ask him to give it back to me.

Once I tried to ask him about his background, but he said, "Crazy background" and I guess I was supposed to know what he meant.

The folks started to joke around with him after a while, which they never did with me anymore, and it wasn't long before he was having lunch in the office with them. I myself dined at a little drugstore on the corner.

He was friendly with them, in that way he had that I didn't like at all, and I could see they liked Mr. Underhill. Called him George.

Within three months you'd think he owned the place, he was so familiar in his manner.

Like that time I came in, early as usual, and saw him and Mr. Norgesand in the front office, laughing. There was an aluminum bottle, or I think they used to call them flasks, on the desk and they had paper cups.

Naturally, I went over and started to take the night-cover off the billing machine, when I heard Mr. Norgesand's voice.

"Hey there, Mac! Can you come in here a minute?"

I said, "Yes sir."

"Mac, how old would you say that biller is, there?" He pointed at the machine.

"I believe it was manufactured in 1925, sir. We bought it brand new then."

"Work all right?"

"Like the day we got it, sir. It's been kept up."

Underhill laughed. He poured out some liquor into a paper cup and passed it to me. I refused, of course. He said: "Man, I thought we'd stamped out AA." and wheezed, all his teeth showing. He had a greenish suit on.

"Like the day we got it, eh Mac? No better, no worse?"

Mr. Norgesand was drunk, and in the morning, too. I just nodded.

"Know what, Mac? They got a new biller on the market. Tell Mac about it, George."

"Crazy biller, man. Electrified. All ya do is plug her in and watch her go. Latest kick."

"Latest kick, Mac. Turns out twice as much work, twice as little effort. Doesn't cost very much; pay for itself in a year, two years. Up to date. Now I ask you, what would *you* do?"

I was about to answer but they were laughing, so I went back to work.

Things like that all the time, that I didn't understand, I mean.

Then, the way it all looped up to this, all that I've mentioned, there was the day I punched in right on time. Not any earlier, as the streetcar ran late. I said "Good morning" to Maggie as per usual but she didn't say anything back, which was all right. I hung up my umbrella and my hat and my overcoat and took off my galoshes and started down the aisle.

Underhill was at my desk like he belonged there, but this was all right too. It was getting to be a habit.

Then I saw it.

All my personal belongings were missing. My brass cuspidor, the THINK sign I kept under glass, the pictures of my wife who died a long time ago and of the horses (I've always loved horses —and never been on top of one, the funny part of it). All gone. Even my special letter-opener that a sailor gave me one night and said he had found it on the corpse of a dead enemy soldier at Okinawa.

Underhill didn't notice me at first, although I was standing right next to him. I watched him awhile.

He was young-looking there in the light, and seemed to be busting with energy like. I wanted to haul off and hit him with something because of the nerve, but I couldn't help for a second admiring that energy. The papers weren't all in order and things were helter-skelter all over, and yet somehow he had done the work pretty well. I'll have to admit that. It was only—he reminded me there of *somebody*, and I didn't know who. For no reason at all, I thought of the joke I'd started a while back, and things got dizzy.

"Mr. Underhill!" I said.

He didn't move. Kept right on working.

"Mr. Underhill, I'm speaking to you. I want you to stop this or I'll have you fired. What do you mean anyway by taking my personal belongings?"

Mr. Norgesand came out of his office, looking sad. He didn't do anything but point at a big black satchel, the one the company had given me some years back and I had always kept in the office. I went and looked inside, by instinct; and there were my things, stacked in neatly.

Mr. Norgesand said "I'm sorry," sighed and returned to his office. Nobody else looked up, Sophie or Joe or Maggie or any of them.

Then I saw the envelope on the corner of my desk, made out to me personally.

It contained inside one month's pay in full.

And nothing else.

And that's about the story, I guess.

I don't even go by the office any more. I used to, though, toward the first, when it got late at night and I didn't know what else to do with myself.

Used to stand there in the shadows thinking all kinds of things, looking up at the window which would be jet-black except for the corner where my desk was.

There would always be a light there.

And I'd see Mr. Underhill—working late.

Resurrection Island

I was trying to talk the receptionist into a weekend at Palm Springs when the call came. It was from Welch. He almost never called: one of those in-at-ten, out-at-eleven bosses—the successful kind. That's why I jumped.

He was drinking milk out of a Martini glass as I walked in. The shades were drawn. Everything was quiet.

"You wanted me?" I asked.

He put down the glass and coughed: Welch had ulcers. "Yes. What are you working on?"

I wasn't working on anything, but you learn to think fast in Hollywood. "The Sinatra thing."

He looked puzzled for a second. Then he said, "Drop it. Turn it over to Mike."

"What's up?"

"I don't know," he said. It was hard to think of this guy as the head of a string of movie fan magazines. He used to be city editor on a New York sheet that folded; then he bought a dying rag somewhere in Oklahoma, and it folded, too; then he borrowed some dough and started *Movie Secrets*. It didn't fold. I guess that's what gave him ulcers. "Artie, I don't know what's up. Maybe something big, maybe nothing at all." He reached across his desk and tossed a tradepaper my way. "I got the rumble from Angelino."

Angelino: that's a four-foot, five-inch newsie on the strip. A little blackmail here, a little informing there. People pity him. They tell him things. He tells us.

I flipped to the page Welch had marked in grease pencil. It contained an ad; not very big, not much different from the others.

EXTRAS WANTED!!!

Ten thousand extras needed urgently by Carl Grushkin. Will guarantee *double* Guild minimum pay ... Many speaking parts ... The chance of a lifetime. Write inquiry, stating qualifications, to Box 304, Los Angeles, Calif.

"You'll be goddamned," Welch said. "Right?"

"Yeah," I said. "I thought that louse was dead."

"So did everybody else." He got up, walked over to the portable bar and returned with a bottle of milk. Half a quart disappeared down his throat. "Well?"

"A gag," I said. Not a funny one, either. Most of the extras in town were starving. Not that things were bad—at least a third of the lots were working—but the pictures were Serious-type. No casts of thousands. No Indian uprisings, no Arab wars, no Atmosphere.

"You think so?"

"Hell yes." It was a typical Grushkin prank. In his day he was probably the best known, most successful director in the world. And I suppose a lot of people were for him, because his pictures were Big, and that meant work. *David* was his first spectacle. You probably remember it: a fantastic, sprawling thing, full of blood and sex and scripture. It cleaned up at the box office. Then came the remake of Griffith's *Intolerance*—five-and-a-half hours on Panorama-scope, location shooting in six countries, $15,000,000 budget. A smash. And then *The Battle of Dunkirk*, which gave a job to every extra in town. Another smash.

But not everyone loved him: only those who didn't get close, who could sit back and chuckle over his 'eccentricities.' A lot of others hated his guts. I was one of them. Never mind why; let's just say that as a fan magazine writer I saw a lot. I called Grushkin Janus in my column once and damn near got fired. But it was true. While one of his faces grinned on the multitudes and uttered blessings, the other arranged for executions. And there were plenty of those. Especially among the weak and helpless, the sick, the disturbed ...

Anyway, the guy made one more picture: *Gettysburg!* It outdid all his others, broke the attendance records from New York to Bangkok, and caused one columnist to write: "With this film, Carl Grushkin has carried the so-called spectacle to its final limits. There is nothing else in the way of realism that could possibly be done with a camera."

"The Creature," as he was called, had announced plans for another movie; then, suddenly, he disappeared. Nobody knew where he went—probably to Africa for some big game shooting, or to Tibet, maybe. He wasn't heard from for over a year.

Then he returned. Looking pretty much his old self, too: cocky, confident, assured; like a five-year-old with a dirty secret.

But, unlike the Grushkin of before, he didn't talk much.

When he bought that island off the coast of Baja and named it *Resurrection*, even then he didn't talk.

And once that immense stone wall was built around the island (it must have been three years ago) there wasn't a peep from him . . .

"Remembering?" Welch asked.

I nodded.

"Still think it's a gag?"

"I . . . don't know. What do you figure?"

"Another spectacle," Welch said, hitting the milk. "Closed set. Hush-hush. Big splash later on. Artie—"

I felt it coming, the way you feel the dentist's drill a second before it hits your tooth.

The Fortune Cleaners was a run-down trap on the wrong side of L.A., across from the trucking joints. I stood in front of it, shuffling my feet, trying to get warm. So did thirty other guys. It was six-fifteen in the morning. At six-thirty a bus was supposed to show.

Getting into the extras' guild was impossible, on such short notice, so I'd had to turn crafty. I knew a fellow named Sandy McLaughlin. He'd been one of the best-paid character actors in the business; then, in that mysterious way, all of a sudden nobody wanted him any more. He'd sunk to bit parts, finally to extra roles. But he didn't like it. When I asked for the loan of his card, he said sure, provided I'd give him what he'd have made off

Grushkin, double SEG. Of course he'd planned to go. So had every out-of-work extra in town. Why not?

After the switch, he filled me in. At a certain time I was to appear at a certain address (they'd phone later) where I, as Sandy, would be picked up and taken to San Felipe, a little village in Baja on the edge of the Gulf.

He also showed me a contract he'd had to sign. The first page read:

> "I, James Andrew McLaughlin, do hereby offer my services as actor to Resurrection Films, Inc.; and in particular, to Carl Grushkin, Producer and Director. I will perform willingly and without coercion of any kind, any and all duties listed on pages four and five of this agreement. Further . . ."

I asked him what the angle was.

"Stunt stuff, I guess," he said. "There was a lot of it in *Gettysburg!* Some people got hurt, they sued—you know. Protecting himself."

"Yeah. By the way, would Grushkin recognize you?" With me, it was a chance.

"I doubt it," Sandy said. "Extras don't have faces, friend. They're just atmosphere."

So he got the call, after a few days, and phoned me. "The Fortune Cleaners. Third Street. Six-thirty a.m. And don't ask me anything else . . ."

I rubbed the smog out of my eyes and walked to the back of the pack. Nobody knew me. At 6:30 on the button, a bus rolled up. It looked like one of the regular city jobs, only painted plain gray. The driver opened the door and got out.

"All right, over here," he said. "Let's do this quick as we can. Have your contracts ready."

We lined up. When I got to the entrance, he took Sandy's papers. "McLaughlin?"

"Yes." Sandy never palled around with the regular extras too much. A snob, thank God.

In three minutes we were on the road.

★

When we pulled into San Felipe, it was nearly midnight. Outside, it looked like day: big moon, lots of stars. I could see twenty or more buses parked on the shoulder by a little cemetery, with about three hundred people milling around. Beyond them, the town itself—a fistful of clay shacks—and beyond that, the black water of the Gulf.

"Follow me," the driver said.

We walked over to the crowd, waited for a couple more buses, then filed down the dusty path through town to the beach.

Three forty-passenger lifeboats were waiting. They filled up fast and glided off, got swallowed by the darkness. Then they came back.

I got on number three, toward the bow.

The oars were quiet as we slid out to sea. Another ten minutes and I saw our destination—*The Gander*, Grushkin's own private yacht. It wasn't as large as Onassis's, but it was large enough. Over a million had gone into it.

The lifeboats came in fifteen times; then *The Gander* upped anchor and we headed due south, into the blackness.

It got cold about then, so I stopped one of the crew, a hefty Mexican. "Any particular cabin?"

He shook his head. Either he hadn't understood or the answer was no.

I found a door and opened it. Inside, four-by-nothing, one bunk, occupied. It was a dame but her back was toward me. "Mind if I use the floor?" I said.

No answer. I rolled my jacket into a pillow and slept like a TV repairman. When the bells started clanging hours later, I woke up and discovered two interesting things. The first was outside the porthole: Resurrection Island half a mile away.

The second was standing over me: one of the most beautiful girls I'd ever seen!

Some women are dumped off the assembly line and other women are hand-built. This one was hand-built, from the ground up. They'd taken special care above the waist.

"Who are you?" she said.

"Sandy McLaughlin."

"That's a lie. I've worked with Sandy."

I gave her the story, then; she shrugged and lit a cigarette. "Maybe you'll write something about me someday, Mr. Wilde."

Her name was Gloria Martin; from Nowhereville, Idaho. Came to Hollywood to be a star, kicked around the offices, landed a few TV jobs, not many, not enough. The usual. Central Casting was inevitable.

"Maybe I will," I said. "You're pretty enough. Got talent?"

"Yes," she said. "But only for acting. And I understand that's only step number one . . ."

"Sometimes. Mostly it's the breaks. I know a lot of dolls with sore behinds who never made it and never will; I know a few of the other kind who are doing okay. Don't get the couch complex."

She looked mad for a second, then she smiled. "I like you, Mr. Wilde," she said. "I don't know exactly why—you're not very good-looking, and you're a little old. But I like you."

"Everybody does," I told her, "for the first five minutes."

We did the silent scene; then somebody knocked on the door and shouted, "On deck!" and that broke it.

"Afterwards?" I said.

She said, "Afterwards."

We joined the gang and got a real look at Resurrection Island.

Alcatraz never seemed grimmer.

The wall was at least fifty feet high, made out of solid concrete blocks. It edged around the whole island, which I figured to be about three miles square. The top was a mess of camouflage —painted canvas, twigs, brush, leaves. People had tried to get in when the news was hot, but no one had ever made it. It was Private Property.

A small guy with a big limp led us up the steps (which had been carved from the boulders) and then he held his hand in the air. Most of the extras were feeling all right, talking softly, giggling, as if they'd each had a couple of whiskies.

Big Limp went over to a huge door and lifted a knocker; it fell with a deep crash.

Next to me, Gloria was shivering a little. There was the sound of logs scraping and hinges groaning; and then, slowly, slowly, the giant door began to open.

Somebody said, "Goddamn." He was right.

Inside the walls there was a set. But it was different from any set I'd ever seen. You kick around the studios long enough, you finally get to tell plaster from brick. There wasn't any plaster here.

Big Limp took us through a smooth field of dust and crushed rock, through a valley of hills and boulders and immense trees; past an amphitheatre that was a ringer for the Roman Colosseum, and finally past the gate of a stone fortress to a clutch of green quonsets.

"You will find your own rooms," he said. "Costumes will be fitted at eleven-fifteen."

Gloria put her hand on my arm. "Would you mind the floor again?" she said. "For some reason, Artie, I'd like to have you around . . ."

We cut out for one of the huts. Inside of an hour we were getting along fine. She talked a lot: I learned all about her family, her dreams, her ambitions, her defenses.

At eleven-fifteen a fat woman asked our sizes.

At twelve she came back with two bundles.

Mine contained a helmet, a shield, a breastplate, and all the other paraphernalia the Roman soldiers were supposed to have worn.

Gloria's was simpler: a gauzy, flowing white dress.

And that pinned it down. Grushkin was going out for the *Quo Vadis* routine. But why all this hanky-panky? Why the cloak-and-dagger methods?

We'd been told to dress right away, so we did. I was given instructions by the girl to turn my head, and damned if I didn't. When she said okay, I turned again and almost dropped my shield.

"You," I said, "are beautiful." I was about to expand on the subject, but I was interrupted by bugles. Then a loudspeaker blared, telling us to assemble in the square within the hour.

"Afterwards," I said again.

Gloria came forward and kissed me on the forehead, very gently. Then on the mouth, not so gently. It told me what I wanted to know.

We followed the others to a square directly beneath the south wall of the stone fortress. The men were in battle uniforms, the women in white dresses. Breakfast was passed out—toast and champagne—and we shuffled around for a while.

Then a single sharp word cut through the air. "Gentlemen!" Every head arced skyward. "Ladies!"

A man had appeared on the topmost battlement of the fortress. He was lean and hawk-like, tall in spite of his slouch. Tan jodhpurs and dark leather boots coated his legs; a black shirt, open at the neck, stuck to his bony torso. And over his shoulders was draped a heavy black coat.

"For the benefit of those who do not know me," he said, into the mike, "my name is Carl Grushkin. I am your employer. I am your landlord. I am your captain. You all have questions, I'm quite sure. And they shall be answered. But not now, not today. Today we must work. Today, my friends, we begin on the most important motion picture ever conceived!"

He did it all in that soft, husky voice I remembered. It had a hypnotic effect. The Legions rumbled, beginning to fall.

Grushkin struck another pose. "It isn't necessary," he said, "for you to have scripts. That is the old fashioned way—" He went on, sonorously, to explain that the greater portion of the film had been completed. All that remained was the key battle scene; and that he would personally direct. Spontaneity, that was what he wanted. Spontaneity. We were to forget we were actors, forget scripts, forget movies.

". . . I am paying you for a job. Your only concern therefore is with the job. I will, however, tell you a few things here and now, quickly. This place is called Resurrection Island. Does anyone know why it is called that?" Dead quiet. "Because, my good friends, what I have accomplished in the past months here will *resurrect* the lifeless corpse of Hollywood! With the release of *this* film, people throughout the world will *stampede* to the theatres

—for it will be something no one has ever seen before. A spectacle? The word is puny. All of the adjectives are puny. They will have to make up new ones for us! *I give you my word!*"

The rumbling grew louder.

"That," Grushkin said, "is our duty. And it is our honor. To restore to the world its most precious possession—entertainment. Are you with me?"

A couple of obvious plants yelled, "Yes! Yes!" and the sheep joined in. "Yes! Yes! Yes!"

A pass from the maestro. Silence. "Then, work with me! Help me! Do as you are told and ask no questions—not for a while. Do you have faith in motion pictures—motion pictures on the large scale, pictures that throb and pulse with life?"

"Yes!"

"Then have faith in Carl Grushkin!"

He turned the excitement up and down as if he were controlling it with a dial. His father had been one of the finest actors on the American stage, and "The Creature" had learned plenty. Even Gloria got lost in the magnetism of the man's personality; and she was a sharp little kid.

"He's delivered that cornball speech before every picture he's ever made," I said.

She didn't hear me.

Now Grushkin was explaining the day's shooting. We were first rank Roman fighters, we men; and the women—

"—will be taken to another section of the set for additional footage."

Pause while the women were separated from us by a crew of flunkies. Gloria squeezed my hand. "I'll see you tonight," she said. "That's afterwards enough. Besides, that floor looks awful hard . . ." For some reason I hung onto her.

"Go on back to the hut now," I said.

She looked at me as though I'd turned purple. "And miss the fun? What's the matter with you, Artie?"

I was about to answer when she pulled away. I watched her and the other women, looking like flocks of white gulls, move off from the square. In moments they were gone.

"Men, you're led by Julius Caesar himself!" cried Grushkin. "Waiting on the field of crushed rock, by the banks of the Sambre, are fifteen hundred crack Nervii warriors. You're to engage them in battle and conquer them!" His voice got tight. "These Nervii are villains!" It got ripe with emotion. "They have worked treachery upon Caesar, whom you love. They are of poor blood. You despise them! And you know, you *know* that they must be thrust back!"

On and on he went, wrapping everyone up in his tale of the battle; then he gave us some technical stuff, where the cameras would be, how to use the weapons, how we should follow everything he said—to the letter.

"And now, my fine Romans, *into the breech*!"

Big Limp led off the yell, and guided us back to the field. The other crew of extras was there. They were dressed differently, but had the same half-wild, half-confused expression. The champagne for breakfast had helped.

A couple of trucks pulled up, then, and some workers started unloading.

The weapons.

Each of us got three items: a broadsword, a club with a flanged metal head, and an ax. And that's when the answers came—not that I was jolted with surprise. The contract, the secrecy, the big routine, the island—everything.

These weapons weren't made out of hard rubber; they weren't plywood or plastic or crystal-candy.

They were real.

I started to move when, suddenly, the air got full of music. Bright yellow martial music, in fast tempo. And a loudspeaker, screeching: "Men, listen! Listen to me! You all have your weapons. You know that they're genuine. The swords will cut and the axes will split and the maces will take a man's head off. And that's my secret. This battle scene *will not be faked*. There will be blood, but it will be real blood. There will be death, but it will be real death. And it will be the most revolutionary thing that ever hit the screen!"

I looked around, trying to find Grushkin. Cameras everywhere, from every angle, but no sign of the director. His voice came from nowhere, from everywhere, over the marching music.

"Men, you have a choice now," he said. "You can call the idea ridiculous, lay down your weapons and refuse to cooperate: that is your right. I can't force you into it, not even with a contract. But if you do this cowardly thing, if you pull out now, what will you do? Go to work in offices? In shipyards? Will you dig ditches for a living? Because the motion picture industry doesn't need you. It doesn't want 'atmosphere' any more—it wants actors. And you're not actors, you're *extras*. Extras! A vanishing breed!"

The voice stopped, but the silence held every man in the field. Only the music roared, above the silence, under it.

Then Grushkin's voice snaked huskily out again. "It's a risk you'd be taking, but I'll pay. To each brave man who survives, whether wounded or whole, *I offer a bonus of one thousand dollars plus a contract without options for two years!*"

The extras screamed. They yelled and hollered and lifted up their weapons. It was fantastic: the music swelling, wild and maniacal now, urging them forward; and these poor guys falling for it!

Someone from the other camp—one of Grushkin's goons—picked up a heavy rock and hurled it. It struck one of our boys in the chest. He in turn picked up a heavier rock. The goon dodged.

The battle was on.

A little music, a phony pep-talk from Grushkin, and thirty-five hundred men were ready to sacrifice their lives!

Then I thought of Gloria, and a chill went down my spine. I got a few steps. Guards at the river; the north and south exits blocked—no choice except to wade through the brawling pack, straight through, and head for the direction they'd taken the women.

It was chaos already; they were bellowing and cursing, and there was the sound of steel against steel. The loudspeaker cried, "Kill! Kill!" over and over. And they started to kill. A guy with a beard in front of me lifted his arm and brought the tip of his ax down on another guy's shoulder. A sword flashed down silver, came up red. I pushed forward. An old man of seventy, at least, turned. His helmet was on crooked and he was grinning through dirty teeth. "You a Roman?" he yelled, brandishing his mace. I told him yes, but he didn't believe me. Instead he raised the mace.

There wasn't anything else for me to do. I rammed the flat of my broadsword against his throat, hard. He gagged and fell over.

It was a goddamn nightmare. These weren't extras any more; they were Romans and Nervii, out for blood.

I kept pushing forward, thinking of Gloria, of my skin, Grushkin, Welch—and I was lucky. Something sharp bit into my arm, but I pulled away in time.

Somehow, out of all this carnage, I managed to reach the square below the fortress.

But I wasn't alone. Two Nervii stood there, grinning, giggling. There was fever in their eyes.

"Let me through," I said. "I don't want to fight."

"*Kill!*" cried the loudspeaker. "*Kill! Kill!*"

The first warrior, a familiar face in old Westerns, snorted, "What are ya, yella bastard?"

"Yeah," I said. "I don't feel so good."

"You gonna feel worse, doll. Come on, Barney!"

They charged and all of a sudden I didn't feel so heroic. I looked back, but that was impossible: I'd have to join the battling throng. I tried a sprint to the left, but the boys had separated. The one called Barney advanced, ax in hand. I let him get closer, then I shut my eyes and swung the broadsword at his legs. The sharp edge went halfway through the bones. Barney squealed and toppled, freeing the sword. The other guy let out a string of curses and came loping. I turned and pelted in the direction of the Colosseum.

He caught me at the entrance, tried to grab, only his fingers slipped on the blood that was seeping from my wound. It wasn't much of a wound, but it saved me. I got my other arm around his throat, tightened, and pulled out the ax.

He just fell and lay still.

I dropped the ax, crept though the entrance and stopped until my heart began to beat anything like normally. Then, because

I didn't want to fight again, because I was tired and sick, I went inside the stone bowl.

It was trading one nightmare for another.

I'd wondered where the women were. Now I knew. They were here, in front of me, in the big clay arena.

What was left of them, anyway. The lions had gotten the rest . . .

It took a while, but eventually I found Gloria. The white dress was mostly red now, and torn to shreds, as her flesh was. A wide-open scar ran down the side of her face.

She was dead.

I hadn't been in love with her or anything. She'd been just a nice girl, and I'd wanted to help her, sure, and sleep with her, too; nothing more. But something happened to me then, looking at the clawed-up mess of dead meat. Something big, and new.

Up to that moment the only person I'd ever really hated was a weak son of a bitch named Wilde. Now I hated somebody else. Now I had a chance to do one good thing . . .

I touched Gloria's hair, once, turned and ran out of the arena, out into the field. And I hoped somebody would get in my way.

No one did. By now the battle was going full-tilt; it had moved from the field of crushed rock to the square. The Nervii were being driven back, their ranks decimated by the Romans.

I spotted him, after a while. Standing tall against the turrets, his lean body—now in Roman garb—angled over, his eyes gleaming, watching, telling the whole story. Grushkin wasn't interested in making a movie. He was simply playing God. God and Caesar and Napoleon and Alexander and all the great and powerful men who ever lived.

I thought of Gloria. Of how she must have felt when the animal jumped at her, when she realized what was going to happen. It wasn't a lion that killed her, I thought. No. It was Grushkin. He killed her, just as he was killing all these other gullible, ignorant people—

"*For Caesar! For Rome!*"

There wasn't any decision to be made. I tried the doors to the fortress first, found them locked; the windows, barred. I circled around and found a tree.

I climbed it, edged out on its highest branch, swung over to a small opening. Sober I'd never have been able to do it. But I was drunk now. Drunk with hate. So I started up the stones.

I got to the top after a couple of years and found a guard waiting. He swung with his sword and took a small strip of skin off my elbow. I wheeled and brought the mace down, hard. And let go of it.

That left me with the sword. But it would be enough, I felt. Down below the tumult was reaching a new pitch of fury. The screams filtered like the wild, idiotic cries of birds; you could hear the cameras, though, in your mind—turning, turning, getting all the blood and death onto film.

At the end of the stone alley, by a turret, stood one of Grushkin's lieutenants. He held a spear and looked pretty embarrassed. Also pretty cold-blooded.

His back was turned, though, and there was a lot of noise. The broadsword went halfway through him. I felt ashamed, but I hadn't any choice: he guarded Grushkin, and Grushkin was killing hundreds.

I went the length of the alley, to the corner, and flattened there. Eight or nine feet away stood "The Creature" and his pet cameraman.

They weren't talking. Just—looking.

The hate bubbled up again, hot and true, and I ran forward blindly. The cameraman whipped around. Too late. Way too late.

Grushkin turned, stared at his man—who lay draped grotesquely across the battlements—then he looked at me. His eyes probed deep.

"You're Arthur Wilde. A writer—"

"That's right," I said.

"What are you after?"

"You," I said, taking a step.

He appraised the situation, saw that I wasn't kidding, wasn't hunting a deal, and grinned. It gave me chills. I don't know why.

"Very nice," he said, "actually. A fine war and then, a duel between the principals. Just like a movie, isn't it, Mr. Wilde?"

"Not quite." His voice had started to lull me: that was the point. By the time I woke up his hand was halfway to his Luger. Almost any other gun has more muzzle velocity. But of course he'd have a Luger. "I wouldn't shout for help, Grushkin."

He nodded. Slowly he unfastened his cape and let it slide down; then, in one fluid motion, he drew his sword from its scabbard. In the softest, weirdest voice imaginable—a voice that told me he'd lost his marbles long ago—he said, "Action!"

Action he got. We slashed and hacked with those heavy swords without drawing blood once. Then I dented his breast-plate and he jumped up onto the wall. He slashed down at me but missed. I joined him.

Despite his famous foil lessons, I soon found out that broad-swords weren't his style. He was getting winded, and after a few minutes it was clear that I could kill him. Only that isn't what I wanted to do. Because with Grushkin dead, the battle would rage on, probably until every man was finished.

He didn't realize his weakness, thank God. His eyes blazed and he roared with laughter every time the steel sang through the air. Then he got a little too confident.

He raised his right arm high, poised for a long chop. I swung my blade and it connected, flat, with his wrist. His fingers spread and the sword clattered loose.

His smile went away.

"Over to the mike," I said, showing him how easy it would be to disembowel him. "Fast. Turn up the speakers. Stop the fight-ing."

"That would be impossible," he said.

"Do it anyway."

He glanced at the glittering steel tip, shrugged and spoke into the microphone. "Men, lay down your arms! Cease—"

It had no effect. He smiled triumphantly. "You see, there's no stopping them."

"Wrong," I said. "There's a way and you know what it is. One word, pal. Good and loud."

The sword touched his neck. He stiffened. "I had not expected such cleverness from a fan magazine columnist. However, it doesn't matter. It is still my finest achievement, all on film."

"Come on!"

He cleared his throat and barked one word into the mike.

"*Cut!*"

And that did it. Like old trick horses, the extras responded to the command and laid down their weapons.

The battle was over.

I must have glanced away, because I was too late to stop Grushkin. He loped over to the highest turret, crawled to the top and stood on the edge. He swayed there a second, and I searched his face; but it wasn't pain I saw. It wasn't surrender, either. I don't know what it was. I don't think he knew himself.

He had fifty feet, straight down, to figure it out . . .

I'm back at *Movie Secrets* now, putting down the facts on Piper Laurie's hidden romance. People don't talk about Resurrection Island any more; they've forgotten the sixteen hundred men and women who died there. It was Big News for a while, sure. Spreads in *Life* and *Time*. Pictures of Grushkin, of me, of the hired goons, the battlefields, the fortress—

But news doesn't stay hot long.

Particularly in Hollywood.

Welch got his story, though, and I got a raise, and I guess that's something. And when the nights get too lonely, there's always Las Vegas.

I mean, there's nothing really wrong with that receptionist. She's a doll, and pretends to understand when I wake up sometimes, screaming.

The Pool

The warm blood of a freshly killed pigeon, his mother explained from the shadowed chiffonier, is what gives the vase its streaky marbled effect and also accounts for its value. The Japanese first made Pigeon's Blood vases many years before Christ's death and people thought only of their beauty; nowadays there are eccentric laws forbidding their manufacture.

In the silken blackness of the room—silken because of the faint moonglow—Paul tensed and then yielded to the image he knew would soon be gone and replaced by another: Slender, disembodied hands grasping a fat grey bird, pressing from the full breast a crimson stream, pressing until the wings no longer fluttered and the silver cup flowed over.

Della twitched and snored slightly. The image vanished, and the words, and for a moment there was only the moon in the corners of the room.

Then Aunt Pearl's voice slithered into being. "*The most beautiful funeral you ever saw . . .*"

By the dresser, over the heating system, the all-steel coffin appeared slowly and the distant hum of cicadas subdued to a thin trail of organ music. Paul closed his eyes and saw it more clearly, opened his eyes but the coffin was still there. White roses adorned its heavy lid and the room became filled with the sweet odor of flowers. Dimly, as though in line caricature, were the rows of people, their heads bowed and some tremulous with softly heard sobbing.

Within the coffin, waxen, stiff, surrounded in snowy satin, lay himself. "Well, there he is," echoed Aunt Dode's lament in militant sadness.

Paul crushed the sides of his cigarette as he watched himself walk, not grieving and mournful, but terrified, to the coffin. He cried a slight low cry as he saw his hand reach out and then withdraw quickly. He had been afraid that if he were to touch that corpse, it would surely leap up at him, eyes blazing, and the dead fingers would claw at his face.

From another corner of the room came a tiny strangulated sound and Paul sank back onto the pillow. The baby whimpered one more time, turned over in its crib, and soon breathed normally.

It had been the girl's strange nearness and the drinks and the excitement—or perhaps the shrimp and onions—that made him see things and hear things and remember the nightmare. Because he hadn't thought of it until this evening and this evening he could think of nothing else; because it had never frightened him before and now he was frightened. He had walked out of the party, the party in his honor, and made no excuses and driven his car very fast down the empty streets, fighting the nightmare; his hands had trembled on the steering wheel all the way home, but with the lights on and the familiar sight of Della and little Greg, then he had had to fight and strain to think of other things.

A cloud passed the moon and the room was suddenly light. Not remembering that in this house there were no softwood panels to squeak, Paul carefully drew down his corner of the covers, swung his legs to the floor and gradually transferred his weight; he left the bed in one swift movement. Where a few minutes ago a casket had hung suspended, was a chair: Paul got from the chair his robe and slippers, padded across to the big French window and listened a final time, glanced at the outlines of his wife and of his child, and stepped noiselessly outside.

The stars were faraway and cold in the night sky, and there was no warmth from the moon's white smudge. Paul dropped his cigarette, crushed it and lit another. The chilled air mixed with the smoke and made it burn his throat.

Quickly, because he didn't want to, he turned and faced the house. There was nothing of symbol in it now, only the brown-painted shingles sitting squat and colorless, beaded with early dew.

He wished that he could feel foolish and childish. After all, he did recognize the half-nightmare hallucinations in his room for what they were. Utterly normal frights, the like experienced by every decently sensitive person alive, at one time or another. Kids with stomach-aches had worse dreams.

He pulled up his collar, for he was shivering, and began to walk. He'd never gotten used to the stillness, and it was particularly oppressive tonight. No automobile could be heard, no muted drone of distant activity, no radio; nor could there be seen a single light. Only the calm agitated sounds of night creatures, and listless wind whispering through trees and foliage, whining across the cuts in the hills, and the dull silver mists close upon the ground.

As he approached the swimming pool, Paul stopped and waited for the dwarf. Soon it would come, hideous, dressed in priest's habit and mounted upon a freak pillar, and screaming, entreating, begging, in the shrill unworldly voice of the deaf-mute. Paul watched and soon the dwarf came; he clenched his fists and presently the image was gone.

There was only the pool. Shafted moonlight fell over it and hid everything but the green shimmering water, nearly still now, only slightly disturbed by the wind. The fence was of the thinnest twists of wire and surrounded the pool invisibly, like a gauze. The water made no sound. And there was not a twig or leaf upon its surface.

The edge of the bed in his room could be seen, and Della had turned; the covers had been thrashed to the floor. The crib was a dark outline.

The coldness of the cement entered his thin leather slippers and he walked on. No other thought would come now: only the remembering. He knew the question it would lead to, the question he'd asked only on infrequent times in the near past—when all the guests had left and he hadn't been sleepy, or on those few odd grey days turning to dusk on the long drive from the studio.

He walked to the fence and put his fingers through the looped wires and looked steadily at the pool's still water. And realized that it was something he'd not been able to do, ever, not since that first time. The dwarf was gone, but the thought remained. Della. God, did he love her anymore?

Four years, he thought. Four years of waiting, working in

traffic agencies, insurance offices, waiting for it: and then, with one little call from an employment agency, the studio job. So what if it meant only forty dollars a week, and running a machine? It was an environment of atmosphere and romance; he would be around people of similar interests. The change alone would make him work all the harder at night.

But then, a little core had begun to hate, to despise all the Brooks Brothers men walking around, doing work he could do with his hands tied behind him, and making fabulous money. The little core hated to see Della sitting in the living room while he worked in the kitchen hours, hours, until morning sometimes, getting the enthusiastic letters from the editors and watching the bills stack up like garbage. It hated to miss any chance that would get Della some of the clothes she needed so desperately, or allow him the time to give his writing the attention it required. One movie sale would bring enough money to allow him to quit his job and give that time to his work—and the evenings to a little living.

The biggest magazine had returned *Wanderer's Shoes* with the best letter of all. Moreso than any of the others, it had given him hope and courage. *Wanderer's Shoes*, his writer friends said, was a story which promised much of the author. Still too 'special,' but the next time! The editor had said as much himself. The next time Anderson would hit print and people would read his story all over the world and love it, be moved by it and say: "Who *is* this guy, anyway? What a great yarn!"

And before beginning on another, already titled—*The Holy Fountain*—had come the idea. It would be fun, for one thing, but neither he nor Della for a moment took it seriously.

The pool, the night, faded for a while as Paul remembered this, and smiled.

Including every dated, crotchety, shopworn situation they could remember, they'd devoted one evening to whipping up a motion picture synopsis. Della had named it, scowling and then laughing with him: *The Gentle Headsman*. Eight pages of ridiculous mystery, together with trick ending, love interest and even dual identity. They'd retyped it on good bond, put it in an envelope and turned it in to the story department of the studio, and promptly forgotten about it.

Then the voice on the telephone, and: "Hello, Anderson! This is Schukin, over at Reading. We got your story, boy. Not bad! In fact, Robson kind of liked it. Maybe we can do something."

Seven thousand dollars was the amount of the check. Then the move into one of the writers' bungalows, a secretary and a salary of three hundred and fifty a week.

Of course, it was then that Della had first begun to mention money. The apartment was so small, and the walls were paper-thin—altogether uninhabitable, she'd said, jokingly.

The powerful subjective passage in *The Holy Fountain* required his undivided attention. He'd tried a few times to get into the story, but there had been constant interruptions—Della asking about how this or that script was coming along, the telephone, constant interruptions, constant.

His serious work could wait a little while, certainly, because soon he could give it its honest due.

More scripts; more sales; more money, yes, but no time, barely enough to scribble a sentence or two or jot down an idea.

At first Della would say, every now and then: "Hey, keed, when ya ever going to finish up the story? Gosh sakes, Burnheim'll forget all those nice things she said about *Wanderer's Shoes* if you don't hit them again soon." She'd say: "We don't want this Hollywood monster to eat us up, do we?" And he'd laugh, and sometimes, late at night when the place was quiet, sometimes he would sit down again at the typewriter. But only nausea, not words or thoughts ever came. And he had put it off to the excitement, which would surely level off. Of course he couldn't write now: things were still in transition.

"Take a tip from your agent, Dad—old Ash hasn't steered you wrong yet. Gather ye rosebuds whilst ye may. You're hot, Poppsy, but things have a way of cooling down mighty fast in this neck o' the woods. Plenty of time for the Naked and the Dead stuff when you've got some real loot. Live 'er up now: way I look at it, if you've got it, you've got it, and a little thing like a cool couple of hundred grand ain't gonna stand in your way."

The sale, the party, the increasing adulation, the diminishing sneers from him and Della. Only once in a while did he get a clear glimpse of the pattern. It had been the way he'd put off explaining to himself about dark cars.

Then there was that drive through the canyon.

They'd driven through it before, in borrowed jalopies which threatened to give up with every turn. This time they drove a low, grey two-seated English car with double spotlights and milkwhite tires. The two-seat arrangement had been Paul's idea.

He remembered Della's face, how it had looked in the steel canyon twilight.

Set upon the newly scraped knoll, the house had loomed up deceitfully: it looked old and earned. With the full new trees and wide dichondra, the stables in the distance and the tiny guest house, it looked almost like a home. The brick was preweathered, as they'd said, the solid wood smoked and hand-hewn to preserve the look of proud antiquity.

The swimming pool was in the rear and he did not see it until Della had been through the house and oh'ed at the spacious luxury, the prewar brass plumbing fixtures, the electronic heat, and the room that would be just perfect for his den. When he saw the pool it was too late.

It didn't have a fence, then. The salesman referred to it casually: "Incongruous, you might say in a way, but who can get along without one these days?"

Paul remembered so clearly, how he had stood transfixed in that sudden petrifying thought, and wanted to leap into the car and never come back to the place. And how Della had looked at him, begging with her eyes: Della, who had endured so much, Della, who was so fragile and heavy with the child . . .

Paul shook his head and searched the pockets of his robe for another cigarette. His hands trembled a bit and he saw that the skin was stretched brittly tight and red.

There was still no sound in the night. He knew that it was only a twenty minute drive, past sleeping homes down the snake road, to life and activity; he knew this, and yet the surroundings became increasingly desolate. He saw, beyond the quaint wooden fence which bounded his acreage, only hills, stark, some of them ragged with burnt brown foliage, all looking lonely and untouched. With the low-hanging mist, it seemed to Paul that he was at the bottom of an eternal silent ocean, down where no living thing had ever penetrated.

He directed his eyes again to the pool. Small gusts of wind had come now and they rippled the green surface into broken lights, unsteadily, dreamily. There was not yet enough for spray, but Paul put his hand to his face and found it wet and clammy. His breath showed faintly in the air.

This was the end of the remembering. Now he would have to face the question, form it, spell it out and not run from it.

He longed for a cigarette.

If only he'd transferred his desires, forgotten about *Wanderer's Shoes* and *The Holy Fountain* and the other moving, important stories that lay lodged within himself, begging pitifully for release. If he'd forgotten them and found happiness in what he now had—others hungered for what was his. Why couldn't he have adjusted? Della had done so nicely...

And why had it hit him so strongly at the party—the party in his honor—so that he was driven to it? The whole commissary full of friends, new friends, the beautiful star Suzan glancing at him with dark, inviting eyes, everybody wishing him well...

The first novel of the distinguished young American short story writer, Paul Anderson, is without question one of the most important documents of this, or any other, generation. The prose is clean and deceptively simple, but in its eminent readability, one never loses sight of the tremendously profound message which underlies every sentence. What Hemingway was to another demand, Anderson is to...

That he'd not betrayed, not, at least, the thought. Its place was hard and lasting, but small as a plant and as easily injured.

He knew the price of what he really wanted, the test that must decide it, and he thought of failing. So much to be learned, so much more to be unlearned; and alone, quite alone, for Della would not go back, not now; for Della did not exist anymore.

The wind grew stronger and the water began an irregular movement: occasionally it would slosh at the sides, then recede.

Suddenly, as the moon shone in the absence of clouds, Paul could look into the water down through the depths to the wavering floor of the pool.

The dwarf sprang from nowhere. And spoke distinctly, with greater insistence and greater insouciance. Paul shuddered as the shadowy dream-creature hopped behind the wire fence.

Paul shook his head violently; the wind caught at his hair. "No!" he said. "No!"

Water had always terrified him: he became hysterical even when his ears touched water. He couldn't swim. And Della was sleeping soundly—and there was the test, the thing he'd feared and fought and now could not escape.

In comparison, sang the emptiness where the dwarf had been, this is a small thing; but it will give you your answer.

The cords in his neck tightened and his muscles quivered; he tried to move, but could not. Images whirled before him.

He'd had the feeling once before, when he was a child and lived in a small town. Every time a train was announced, he would run to the depot and would wait there until the rumbling black speck appeared, spitting sparks and dirty smoke, hurtling with great speed along the dull tracks, growing larger and larger, blowing and screaming like a crazed elephant. He'd had the feeling then: To wait until the train had roared almost parallel with him, then to hurl himself across the tracks! How he'd fought that urge, bit his dry tongue, never really knowing what he'd do until, in an eternal second, the train had coughed quiet and then strained off again.

He walked from the pool, back to the French window and into the bedroom. Della lay on her stomach, with her face mashed grotesquely on the pillow. She breathed regularly.

He walked past his wife to the end of the room and stopped at the crib; and felt the knots in his temples about to burst.

The infant was curled with its legs drawn under and its face to one side. The fine hair was golden in the shaded light.

Paul felt suddenly weak, and he was afraid that he might tremble and waken the child. But steadily he scooped it into his hands, slowly and with calculated movements. It did not stir when finally he had it in his arms; and he let the held breath escape his lips in a long stream.

Della squirmed and half-lifted her arm, then dropped it back to the bed. There was a slight noise, but then a great quiet once more.

He went out of the bedroom and back to the cement walk. The air was cold: he lifted the skirt of his robe and gently placed it around the child in his arms.

He heard the dwarf rustling and mumbling, and bent to unlatch the door of the fence. He thought of water rushing into his ears and covering his eyes, the cold water of the pool, how it would part greedily and receive its helpless victim—and then close again. How its placid shimmering greenness would mock and invite him, afterwards.

If I lack this courage, he thought, how could I hope for the other? And a thin voice echoed him.

Paul walked steadily to the edge of the pool. The infant opened its eyes and closed them and made a tiny sound.

Straining, to keep from trembling, he let the robe fall back and held out his arms, so that the child was suspended directly above the water of the deep end. The weight increased and he felt his muscles failing: hot wet flames blinded him as the dwarf, and millions of dwarf-creatures, pressed forward, clutching the child he held, pulling, tugging.

All the sounds of the infinitesimal night things seemed to stop and there was only the whisper of the water as it sloshed against the sides of the pool; and the wind from the hills, damp and sickly.

Paul reeled once and took one step forward, then the tears broke from his eyes and he pulled the baby back to his chest. He held it there tightly and it cried out when he turned, finally, and stumbled to the bedroom. Controlling himself, he put his small son back into the crib and watched until sleep returned and the settling movements had stopped.

He looked out one time only at the pool, which was now turning grey with the sun; at the empty hills and the sky of old clouds: once he looked.

In a little while the dancing colors faded into iron black and he dreamed a faint distant dream.

He stood in a large square room, which was bare and littered with the debris of many years: years of undisturbed dust lay upon the debris. But the room was not quiet. It was filled with a wild rustling and pinched cries; there were sharp sounds too, from time to time.

In his dream, Paul saw two windows in the room, side by side. One was open, and wind set the ragged lace curtains undulating: the other window was closed, puttied, nailed, and dust lay caked over the seams.

Suddenly the room became alive. The sounds took shape and he saw many doves, spotless, fragile. The doves were fighting frantically for escape.

Before the dream closed into fitful darkness, Paul heard and saw the wild white birds flying again and again at the closed window, hurling their bodies at the grimy glass, some falling to the floor, some merely crying and fluttering their wings.

But all avoiding the open window.

Fallen Star

The road to Palm Springs, which is Hollywood's Heaven, passes through a grey purgatory of food stands (AVOCADOS NINE 4 $1.00!), freak shows (SEE THE MONSTERS OF THE DESERT! UNBELIEVABLE! CAMERAS WELCOME!) and the ugliest, saddest mountain in the world. Usually I hurry by that mountain. This time I stopped. In the hot sunlight I stopped and stared at the heaped-high tower of rusted metal, at the countless mangled, crushed and forgotten skeletons of what had once been cars. Each part of that eroding hill had been a bright possession, once: new paint, new smell, new feel. *Well, what do you think of her?* I almost heard the voices, there in the silent desert noon. *Say, now, that's really something! . . . Gonna take her to the Springs and let her out! . . . Be careful!* Then, still standing in the shadow of that metal mountain, I began to hear the frightened-woman screech of brakes, the swirl of headlights—*Jesus!*—and the muffled thunder of the cars, which had been aimed a dozen years before, colliding.

Mostly, though, I thought: There'd be no mountain here if things stayed young, if things stayed new.

I realize, now, why I stopped; I didn't then. Annoyed, I climbed into my young, new Porsche Speedster and took off. The furnace-blast of air, beloved by Southern Californians, made my head ache. The sun blinded me. Why had *I* been singled out, I wondered, for this job? Why not Jim Gaskins, who loved writing profiles, who delighted in asking impudent questions of vapid actresses?

You'll see, my editor had said.

But, I had told him, I don't even own a television set! I don't know a damn thing about it.

That's why I'm sending you.

You're crazy! What'll I say?

You won't say anything. You'll listen.

Look, goddamnit, I write fiction. I may have a contract with your magazine, but that doesn't mean you can—

Shut up. Ruby Nelson is the biggest thing in show business. The most popular actress in the world today. She lives in Palm Springs. That's all you need to know. Go get me a story.

But—

But, but, but. Ralph had done me so many favors, I couldn't turn him down. However, it was true: TV was a world unknown to me. I wasn't angry because of any feeling of superiority; it was simply that I was frightened. Most fiction writers are that way.

The grubby little towns fell back. The crippled palm trees disappeared. Soon I was in the desert, and this was frightening, too. Because suddenly you look from your speeding car, which only a couple of hours ago was creeping with the flux of Los Angeles traffic, and you see desolation. Emptiness. You see a bush-pocked plain of tan and gray, bone-dry, board-dry, dry past the help of rain; a sprinkle of ancient stones; and beyond, the purple mountains, false, unreal, like flats of papier-maché. And you think the old cliche, if you're like me: that all this was before you were, will be when you are gone. And who the hell would want to be reminded?

Not out of the desolation, then, but into the city that had been an Indian village: carved, as they say, out of the wilderness. Palm Canyon Road. On either side, motels. Each with a swimming pool. Each with TV. EL MIRADOR, THE DRIFTING SANDS, TRANQUILLA, DESERT PARADISE.

The shops. The real estate buildings. The great finned Cadillacs. The Hawaiian-shirted businessmen and their bikinied loves.

Civilization.

I drove into a Standard Station and asked where 10789 Mira Vista was. The station attendant told me, and the perspiration started, then.

The house was one of those low sprawling "desert-ranch" homes, painted yellow. The flat roof was covered with rocks. I parked my car at the curb and forced myself to wonder specifically what I would say. Ralph had given me no warning. I'd had a chance to see only a portion of one of Ruby Nelson's films, and

I knew that she was a beautiful girl and a good actress. I didn't know anything else about her.

The door opened before I was halfway across the sidewalk. I heard the sort of voice that pushes up through dirty filters:

"You're late."

A woman stood at the doorway, swaying slightly. She looked attractive at first, clad in a bright yellow sweater and tight black shorts, red hair loose around her shoulders, legs firm and naked. There was a martini glass in one hand and a cigarette in a long cigarette holder in the other. Then I got a little closer.

In Southern California, all women are beautiful—from a distance. You see them sweep by in their Thunderbirds, sunlight glinting on their nutbrown shoulders, and you chase them. If you're lucky, you don't catch up. Because they're usually disappointing. The wind flicks back their deep raven hair and instead of the frost-lipped pouting beauty you expected, there's a middle-aged woman with warts.

This woman was more than a disappointment. As I came close to her, the girl I saw from thirty yards vanished. In her place was a female of perhaps fifty, Indian-tan but also Indian-wrinkled. Her eyelids were puffed and red, and the eyes beneath were moist, focusing, searching, squinting against the powerful sun.

"I said, 'you're late!'" The kind of voice that comes of twenty years of day-time drinking; no music, no expression; just a group of vibrations spiraling into inaudible squeaks at anything over bass.

"I'm sorry, I didn't know there was a definite time."

"My ass you didn't." She took a swallow of the martini. "Well, what are you waiting for? Payment in advance?"

She turned and walked back into the house. After a moment, I followed. The interior was what they call Chinese-Modern, a lot of black furniture with gold striping, bamboo chairs, a white rug.

"What the hell are you looking at?"

Her body was almost obscene; it had the firmness and the curves of youth. But there was nothing youthful about her. The shapely, muscular legs did not prepare you for the loose-fleshed arms, the flame-tipped claws, the seamed and ravaged battle-ground of a face.

"Are you Ruby Nelson?" I asked.

"No, Shirley Temple," she said, grinning, showing fine white caps. Then the grin disappeared. She put the empty glass down on a coffee table, walked over and pressed her body against mine. The smell of alcohol was overpowering. I stepped back. She slapped me, hard.

"Get out of here," she said.

I started for the door. Then I turned and saw her standing in the middle of the rug. Her face was red.

"Wait," she said.

She strode to the door and locked it, then she pulled the blinds together. The room went dark. She walked to the mahogany bar, took out a bottle of Beefeaters gin and filled two glasses. One of the glasses she gave to me, and drained the other.

"Come on."

She pulled me to the vast black couch. Then she lay down in what should have been a seductive pose and unbuttoned her sweater.

"They're still good," she said.

I didn't move. I could only sit there, staring at her.

She clutched my hands and pressed them to her bosom. "Still good," she said. "Not so old. Laddie, please. Don't look at me. Take me. Laddie, please."

Her eyes were closed now.

I took my hands away. She cried, "For God's sake, what am I paying you for?"

"Nothing," I said. "There's a mistake. My name's Kelly. I was sent here to interview you."

"Interview—" She began to laugh. It reached a sort of choked hysteria, and stopped. "Well, you got more than you expected, didn't you?"

"I'm sorry," I said. "I didn't mean to embarrass you. I'm new at this sort of thing."

"So am I," she said.

"Maybe I better leave."

"No. I don't want to be alone now, Mr. Kelly. You'll be safe."

She rose from the couch and opened the drapes.

"Palm Springs," she said, "is full of whores. Young men. They rent their bodies to lonely old women. Isn't that disgusting?"

"I guess so."

"Oh, it is. I never tried it before. I'm not so old, Mr. Kelly, listen; but I am lonely. Dear God, yes! I am lonely."

"Why?"

"Because of her," she said. "Because of that filthy miserable little bitch."

"Who?"

She looked at me, then went into the bedroom and came back with a photograph. "Her."

The photograph showed a sweet young girl with the air of the twenties about her, a beautiful girl, large-eyed, supple, dark against white tennis briefs, so innocent, so very worldly.

"You really don't know?"

I shook my head.

"All right," she said. "Have another drink. I'll tell you about it."

The End Product

Joseph MacElroy had been with the Company more years than anyone could remember. He did his work competently and without brilliance, arrived promptly at nine in the morning and straightened up his desk never earlier than five twenty-nine. He was a very old man and so little inclined towards conversation that he never did have a friend in the office, though there was no one who disliked him. He was never known to smile.

As a matter of fact, so much of an institution had he become that the office manager, Mr. Harry Zullock, was deeply shocked to discover old "Mac's" first mistake. It was a small one, a few cents off in an adding machine tape, but even so it could not have been more surprising had it been more serious. Because it had simply never occurred to anyone that Mac could make an error.

Of course, nothing was said to him about it.

But then came the second mistake, requiring much time to remedy, and then the third. And it was decided that Mac should be reprimanded.

"Mac," the manager said one day, "you've been with us a long time and, speaking for myself, you've done your work well. But lately you've been slipping up—" here the mistakes were explained—"and I wish you'd keep a closer eye on those figures."

Mac looked up and said that he couldn't understand how they had happened and that he'd be more careful in the future.

The surprise in the old man's face was the first emotion that Mr. Zullock had ever noticed, and it affected him strongly. He went home that night and thought about it.

And he thought about it more and more over the following month and a half, as old Mac's work got progressively worse. There was no sign of sloppiness or lack of initiative: it was simply that errors were being made.

Which made the situation frightful. Because Mr. Zullock, for all his authoritative power, began somehow to feel a little afraid

169

of Mac. And although he had never before felt hesitant about becoming severe with an erring employee, still it seemed almost sacrilegious to continue reprimanding the old man. To consider relieving him of the position was a thought which had entered Mr. Zullock's mind but which was hasty in its withdrawal.

Clearly a crisis was at hand. And for one unused to crises, such a thing can be unnerving.

At ten o'clock one morning Mr. Zullock looked up from his sight drafts and frowned, because he couldn't concentrate. His office force was a very good one and he knew it and it disturbed him mightily to find any constant note of inefficiency. It was a failing in responsibility.

He looked about the small office.

There was Anne, talking on the telephone to some friend. She made personal calls, but she did her work well so it didn't matter.

Bob Lineman was calling off a tape to John Tommerlyn. There was an efficient pair for you.

Jim Schott, the rate clerk, was on the phone; Norma Bothel was working the addressograph. Good workers.

And all the rest of them, turning the wheels of the Company. What *was* the matter?

Mac. Old Mac. Wearing the same brown suspenders and the same blank expression, his lips moving silently to the papers on his desk.

Mr. Zullock frowned again. Those were important papers, extremely important, and Mac had made two serious and costly mistakes in the past week.

A watch repair man replaces a worn out spring, doesn't he, when the spring ceases to function properly? Yes, a watch repair man does that.

Mr. Zullock sighed and attempted to work on his drafts. But the numbers lost themselves and he kept thinking of long overtime hours and responsibilities and other things.

He pushed the papers aside and walked over to Mac's desk.

"Well, how's she coming?"

The old man turned his head around slowly.

"What was that, sir?"

"Just wondered if everything was going okay. That's a complicated bunch of stuff you've got to untangle, what with the strike in 'Frisco and all."

"I will have it finished directly, sir, and you may check it if you wish."

"Yes, you might give them to me when you're through, if you want, just to make double-sure. Lot of accounts are getting finicky as hell these days, y'know. Minneapolis Mining would drop us like a hot potato if they ever got overcharged for a haul."

Mr. Zullock looked down at the tips of his shoes for a while and then returned to his desk feeling strange.

From the corner of his eye he watched Mac. Watched those wrinkled, brittle fingers move laboriously over the keys of the adding machine and the thin lips working silently. He watched the blank lines of the face and especially the slow cold eyes.

He then noticed the hum of the machines in the office, which he'd never noticed before, so he went into the wash room.

He smoked a cigarette there and thought about many odd things. About God and what fun it might be to draw pictures for a living and who first invented the wheel.

Mostly he thought about the old man who worked for him. He tried to imagine Mac at the age of twenty or thirteen, of what he did when he got home and where that home was, if he kept pets and what his mother looked like.

Then Bob Lineman came into the wash room, looking hot and red as he always did.

"Harry," he said, "why don't you get that damned air conditioner fixed? It's nearly ninety in there."

"Oh, that thing's been out of whack since the day we got it installed. And since we're on the subject of things out of whack, did you ever get that Billings deal unfouled?"

"Where you been? That went through days ago—and believe me, I worked like a dog on that mess."

They laughed. But Mr. Zullock was worried.

"Bob, do you have any idea who it was pulled that boner? You know, we almost lost the account."

Bob started to wash his hand carefully.

"Look, Harry, I've been with the Company five years and next to Johnny I'm the youngest one here. I know who snafued the works, sure. I know who's been pulling 'em right along. But I just don't figure I've got the right to get anyone in dutch, that's all. Just let it ride."

Mr. Zullock's heart began to beat fast.

"It was Mac, wasn't it?"

"Forget it, will you? I took care of it; it's all right."

Mac, again.

Mr. Zullock said nothing and lit another cigarette. Bob Lineman washed his hands again.

"Bob, don't go blaming yourself. I've been noticing a lot on my own hook and I don't like it. And The Boss won't like it either."

"I don't want to butt in, Harry, but, well, since you know why don't you face it? Mac's just running down, that's all. I would too if I was his age; so would you. And what the heck, the union'll kick in something, there's his pension and for all we know he's got a nice little nest egg stashed away in the bank. Probably does—what would he spend money on?"

Silence.

"Look, sir, like I say, I don't want to butt in. It's your business, strictly. But, honest to God, I'm fed up with fixing the old boy's butches. I got my work to do, we all do. And how are we—"

"All right, all right. Don't you think I know? Don't you think I realise what's got to happen? You'd better get back to your desk."

Bob Lineman left, feeling hurt and ashamed and wondering what he'd said to make his boss angry.

As the door opened and closed Mr. Zullock heard the machines. They sounded loud and a chill went down his back.

Mr. Zullock sat down at his desk and began to doodle on a scratch pad. But he could only listen.

The slow deep sound of the machines. Like sad music, the kind they play at funerals.

Cleketah. Cleketah. Cleketah.

Like a slow, infernal dirge.

He looked at Jim Schott. Jim had been with the Company thirteen years, the best rate clerk in the business. He had a wife and two kids and one grandchild. He took vacations and told jokes.

But he was telling them less frequently now and tending more to work. A good sign, The Boss had said.

Who ever heard of keeping a bad spring in a good watch?

I want to be an artist, Mother.

Miss Ten Eyck. With the Company almost eleven years, hadn't missed a day.

Her eyes. *What was the matter with her eyes?*

No one laid off, no one new hired in . . . how many years?

You're going to be an essential part in this great machine, Harry Zullock.

Why did Anne look so different now? She used to slump in her chair but now she sits straight and her personal calls get fewer.

Cleketah. Cleketah. Cleketah. Cleketah.

Quickly Mr. Zullock took a sheaf of papers from his desk and stared at them. They were the manifests Mac had done, the ones he was to check.

Maybe they'd be all right. God, let them be all right!

He wiped his forehead with a handkerchief and began to run through the figures.

2,093. 5,648. 13,257.

Right so far.

3,907. 5,248.

5,248—that couldn't be. It was too much, surely.

He checked against the original copy.

3,248. A difference of two thousand dollars, and on the third set. Only the third set.

Carefully he checked through the seven long, closely printed pages of numbers. There were ten errors: an overcharge of three thousand, eight hundred dollars.

His fingers trembled. If those sheets had gone through the

Company would have lost a five thousand dollar per week account. One of the best accounts.

Mr. Zullock's throat turned dry. He looked from one machine to another, from one worker to another, and he became confused. The roaring hum seemed to grow louder and faster. The machines sang furiously as he'd never heard them sing before.

And soon he could not see the workers at all.

Only dimly could he see the thing he'd been trained over a lifetime to see. But he saw it.

He got up stiffly, took the sheaf of manifests and walked to Mac's desk. The old man was bent over his adding machine.

"Mac," said Mr. Zullock, "I'd like to see you for a minute. Would you come over to my desk, please?"

Mac said nothing. His head did not turn.

Mr. Zullock waited, but there was no response. He waited for a long time and his throat began to ache.

"Okay, Mac, I'll be short and frank. There've been complaints and this manifest you did is a mess. What have you got to say?"

Mac said nothing. His head did not turn.

"Maybe you're run down from so much work, I don't know. But there's too much at stake here to risk any more bungling. Do you hear me?"

Mac's fingers worked slowly over the keys of his adding machine. But he didn't turn his head and he didn't say anything.

The roar of the machines grew louder and louder and Mr. Zullock felt sick in his stomach.

"Times have changed, MacElroy. New methods, new adjustments. You've been too slow; too many mistakes. Do you understand?"

But the only sound Mr. Zullock heard was the *cleketah, cleketah* of his machines.

Mac's fingers barely moved on the keys now.

"Look, I'm talking to you! Why don't you answer? Can't you understand—I'm firing you, Mac. You got all the chance in the world but you fell through. We've got to replace you."

Mr. Zullock was shouting now and he realized it. Something stabbed at his heart. His body shook and he was desperately afraid to look about him. The others—they were watching and wondering.

Like he was wondering. Why he was afraid and why Mac just sat there.

Then the noise stopped, abruptly as though it had never existed. A tomblike silence, tense and expectant. He'd experienced it before; what office worker had not? The sound and the silence, like a person suddenly gone deaf.

He stared at Mac.

An almost imperceptible movement in the fingers and the head turning slowly, slowly.

Mr. Zullock put a hand to his mouth to keep from screaming, when he looked into the eyes of Joseph MacElroy.

And then he did scream, when he heard the soft, uneven sound of one machine.

One machine which clicked for a few moments and was then silent.

The Philosophy of Murder

Mary Ellen Ross had been asleep only a few hours, when she found herself suddenly quite awake and with the overwhelming sensation that she was not alone in her bedroom. Instinctively she told herself that it was just a nightmare, or the mystery film she'd seen that night at the Palomar. But even so, she almost stopped breathing and listened for any unnatural sounds. There were none. Only the creaking of the old house and the dying murmur of what was left of the traffic on Broad Street. That was reassuring but she became frightened again when she remembered that her parents were spending the night at the Johnsons' and wouldn't be back until late the next evening. Jim Johnson and his wife had known Mary's folks for over twenty years and had invited them to another of their parties. Mary was invited too, but then, Stantonville was almost sixty miles away and Leonard Kline had asked her for that date weeks and weeks ago. A wonderful fellow, Len, and a fellow with a future. Not like that terrible Ronald Mansfield, always trying to pet her and always getting mad when she wouldn't let him. Thank goodness she'd gotten rid of *him*!

The room was very quiet and the creaking had stopped, as it sometimes did. But Mary couldn't get rid of that feeling. It scared her and she felt like hiding under the covers. Oh, I'm acting like a silly little girl! There's no one here. I'm practically nineteen years old and besides, there hasn't been any trouble in this neighborhood for simply years. See, now I can't get back to sleep. I wish the street cars were running, or that Len would call up. Ta dum da dee, it's rainin' violets. . . . Wish it was morning already.

She tried not to think of those stories Ronald Mansfield used to tell her. He had once taken a course in criminal medicine, on a scholarship at the University of Zurich. They were horrible stories, stories about girls' bodies in big glass bottles and about men who'd been run over by trains and.... ta dum, it's the silly old moon. She'd asked him not to tell her those things. He'd actually seen the body of that little girl who had a crucifix carved in her stomach, and who.... Those mystery pictures are sure corny. Everybody knew it wasn't the butler. Everybody. Everybody. Everybody. With all her diamond rings, St. Louis woman....

A car passed in the street below her window. The headlights traveled from the ceiling across the wall and over Mary's bed, and then disappeared. The room was blacker than before. But it was no longer quiet.

From the corner where her dressing table stood, Mary could hear something. Something that sounded like heavy breathing. She began to perspire and listened closely. It didn't stop. Unable to make a sound, she buried her head in the pillow. She was trembling and very cold. It isn't anything, it isn't anything, it isn't anything.

As she whispered these words aloud, she heard the shades being pulled down and felt herself blinded when the lights flashed on. She gave a frightened little cry as she felt the covers being pulled from her shoulders. When she forced herself to look she saw a young man standing at the foot of her bed, the covers still in his hands.

He looked at Mary and smiled nervously. He was a lad of about twenty, well dressed, closely cropped hair and with a certain scholarly appearance. He stood there, looking at Mary, knotting the bedclothes in his pale hands.

"Ronald Mansfield! What are you doing here? You get out of here right now or I'm going to call the police. I'm going to tell your mother and father. Get out of my house this very second!"

She recognised her visitor, but was none the less frightened. Ronald was in her morning class at school. She'd gone out with him a few times, but never really liked him. He was always looking at her *that* way, like he wanted to make her. She'd let him kiss her, but it never went beyond that. He'd go telling it to one of his brainy friends and soon everybody would know about it. He'd always get mad and sulk around or come begging for another chance. Then Leonard came along. He wasn't an "A" student, but he could be serious minded sometimes, and sometimes be a barrel of fun. He didn't go around quoting Schopenhauer and saying how terrible the world is and looking at her *that* way, like Ronald did. Ronald was a philosophy major and had it all worked out that the world was no good and everybody in it was no good. He'd even get in big arguments with Professor Warum. Anyway, he was never any fun. Always asking her up to his place to listen to Mahler and Schönberg and look at his library, and to read his silly novel. Ha! Len's such a baby, in a way—he was almost shaking when he kissed her for the first time. That was fun. And she let Len do just about everything he wanted. He knew where to stop. But Ronald. . . . why did she ever get mixed up with him? He wasn't good looking. Looked like a Nazi, with his hair cut short like that. Talked like one, sometimes. Like the time he bragged he'd make a perfect concentration camp officer. Screwball guy. Shorter than she was too. Maybe it was his manners. When you first got to know him he couldn't be more courteous. Always holding the door open and saying "Oh, I beg your pardon, I'm terribly sorry." That was just a show, she soon found that out. Oh, he was smart all right; got the best grades in his classes, even from Prof. Warum. The first night he took her out he gave her a leather bound edition of *Wuthering Heights*. Must have cost him a lot, either that or he stole it somewhere. She wouldn't put it past him. Dressed up in his dark blue suit with that Tartan tie, no clerk would stop him. Not if he gave him one of those serious looks, like he sometimes gives people. And with those horn-rimmed glasses. The second night he was able to get his father's car and drove her home, after the concert. But he came within a block, under that big elm, stopped the car and started to tell her that she was the only thing that could save him. Oh brother, what a line! "You haven't the intelligence to understand what you mean to me," he said. She didn't like that, but let him kiss her. He got real excited and started to pet around. She pushed his hand away and gave him the story about that sort of thing only leading to another, and that she didn't go in for it. It was unsophisticated, but always worked. But not with Ronald.

He kept trying and finally got sore. Then he frowned and drove her home without saying goodnight. She decided not to see him any more after that, but the next day he said he was sorry and begged her for another chance. He seemed to have plenty of cash (even if he did work weekends as a shoe salesman), and after all, that book was a nice present. So she decided to go out with him again. When she met him that night she had on her white suit with that thick, tight belt. It gave her more curves. She was one of the prettiest girls in town, and she knew it. Ronald picked her up at eight thirty, but instead of driving to the theatre he went into the country, near the ocean. He drove for two hours, telling her about his criminal medicine course and telling her that they were going to a party at the house of a friend of his. Then when they were almost to Laguna, he stopped the car and saw that this was the place. She couldn't see any lights and could hear the ocean beating against rocks. She became frightened. He took her hand and they walked down a sandy path. Then he pointed ahead of him, and she could make out the outlines of an old, dark house. What had once been a very large house. The outside was nothing but charred timber, and in the moonlight she could see the edge of a cliff directly beyond. Ronald explained that he thought she'd appreciate his little joke, that he thought only she, of all his friends, could understand the serenity and beauty of that abandoned house. She got angry and scared and began to cry, and when he tried to put his arms around her she ran back to the car. He drove all the way back to town saying he was sorry, that he just wanted to share something with her. She jumped out of the car when they stopped for a signal, and took a bus home. She didn't speak to Ronald Mansfield again in school and went out of her way to avoid him. But he never took his eyes off her.

"Ronald, I'm warning you. I'll call the police. Stop standing there, and give me back my covers. You've certainly got your nerve! Wait till Mr. and Mrs. Mansfield hear about this little trick! Ronald, do you hear me!"

"Mary, I came because I had to. Don't you understand, I came because there was no other way out, I had to."

He dropped the covers to the floor and locked the bedroom

door. Mary was sitting on her bed, trembling and crying. As she saw the young man turn and start toward her, she covered her breasts with her hands. She had on a pair of blue pajamas, the same old pair her grandfather had given her years before. But she felt naked and ashamed and very frightened.

"Surely you know that I've wanted you since the first day I saw you. Why did you have to go on treating me like that, when you *knew* how I felt? I wish I had the courage of Richard Cory. . . . I wished it then. Mary, I was going to ask you to marry me! I told you things I've told no one before. I stripped my soul in front of you. I let you read my novel, I . . . I haven't been able to work on it, Mary, and do you know why? Because of you. I've dreamed of holding you close to me, of feeling your warm body next to mine. . . ."

"Ronald Mansfield, if you don't stop I'll scream. I'll call the police and have you arrested if you don't get out of here!"

"You're beautiful, Mary. More beautiful than any other living creature in this ugly world. I love you as much as I'm capable of loving anyone. Have you any idea of how beautiful you are right now, sitting there with your hair in curlers and all the make-up off your face? Every night I've dreamed of seeing you like this."

Mansfield drew from his coat pocket a small knife. As he pressed a button with his thumb, the blade sprang out.

"This is sharp, Mary. I could kill you with it. I don't want to do that, but I think you know by now that I'm not incapable of such a thing. You mustn't underestimate me. You must fulfill my dreams, or I shan't be able to go on. Is it so great a thing to ask, Mary? But I warn you, if you try to scream or make any noise whatever I'll put this shiny blade in your throat."

He sat on the bed next to Mary and began to unbutton the top to her pajamas. Tears were running from her eyes and she was too frightened to move. He pulled her hands away roughly, holding the knife to her neck, and undid the cord around her waist. Mary began to sob aloud as her naked body was pushed over the bed, and then she screamed at the top of her voice.

At breakfast the next morning Ronald Mansfield kissed his mother and chided that the coffee was not quite up to her standard. He ate heartily, made a final adjustment on his bow tie, collected his books and arrived at the university three minutes early. Later, as the professor lectured on inductive logic, no one noticed that Mary Ellen Ross was absent from her seat. It was certainly not the first time. The professor droned on for two hours. After that followed a general examination in British Empiricism, in another part of the building. Then came a course in Kant and time for dismissal. The final class dispersed and each student left the university, each thinking his own private thoughts.

Later that evening Mr. Gerald Mansfield received a call from the police. Was his son Ronald at home? Would they both please come down immediately to the precinct station? A terrible thing had happened. A young girl, known to have been a friend of Ronald Mansfield's, had been found a few hours ago raped and murdered. Mr. Mansfield said that he would be right over with his boy, he was very shocked to hear such a thing. He went into his son's room.

"Ronald, the police have just called up. It's a terrible thing, but you know that young girl you took out a few times last month? Well, son, she's been found in her home, murdered."

Ronald Mansfield looked up from the book he was reading.

"Mary Ellen? Of course, she was in my class! Good God, Dad, what a thing to happen! Why, I saw her only last Friday."

"They want us to come down to the station. I guess because you knew her. Lord, I pity her poor parents. Well, get on your coat, and I'll get the car."

It was raining slightly and the streets glistened. As they got into the car Mr. Mansfield put an arm around his son's shoulder. "Buck up, my boy," he said for some reason. Then, in a strange tone:

"You were seeing a lot of this girl, for a time, weren't you, son?"

"Yes, Dad, I was. But we found we had no real interests in common, and, well, you know how that goes."

They drove off without saying anything further.

In the station there were assembled all the fairly close friends of Mary's that her parents knew about. There was Amy Lindstrom, Kathleen Farrell's roommate. She and Kathleen and Mary used to see a lot of one another. Kathleen was out of town. There was Pat Davidson, a girl friend, and Marcy Stevens. Marcy and Mary had been old friends. In the corner stood the very pale figure of Leonard Kline. Everyone knew he and Mary had been sweethearts. And sitting down, with his head in his hands, was Tony Sudor, a new student at the University and a new member of the community. He had taken Mary to a dance the week before.

Ronald Mansfield walked over to Mrs. Ross, who was sobbing violently, and put his hand on her shoulder.

"You don't know me, Mrs. Ross, but I was a friend of Mary's. I can't tell you how sorry I am about this. I was just told, myself, and I know what a shock it must be to you."

★   ★   ★   ★

The only one in the group who spoke was Professor Corneille. He cleared his throat nervously, and said in a voice rather too blasé, "Good Lord, James, you can't stop there. Now that you've started this . . . singularly lurid tale, you've got to finish it."

James Morley put out his cigarette and slowly sipped his scotch and soda. Those at the cocktail party, which had begun so gregariously, were listening in rapt silence to the story being told to them. No one thought it possible that the distinguished author and philosophy professor, James Morley, could be capable of such a yarn. And somehow, disturbingly, certain parts of it sounded vaguely familiar to a few of the seated listeners.

"See here, old man, you've admittedly been rattling on like a narrative from some detective magazine, but hang it! what *did* happen? It was easy enough, I suppose, for the police to apprehend this Mansfield fellow."

"No, Professor, the story takes a rather ironic turn at this point. Perhaps its ending will justify the somewhat melodramatic fashion in which I've chosen to tell it so far."

Morley gulped down his drink and poured another. Not a person moved.

"You see, for some unaccountable reason the police suspected young Tony Sudor, who had been in town only a couple of months. It was found that he had once been in a reformatory, on a morals charge. It was discovered that he collected knives as a hobby. And most important, Sudor could not remember where he had been on the night of the crime. Out walking, he thought, he wasn't sure. Astonishingly enough, a witness testified that she'd seen him in the Rosses' neighborhood shortly after midnight. He had no alibi at all, and when they got hold of his diary they found plenty of motive. Well, his lawyer thought a confession would make it easier on him. But by this time the case had heated the public's blood; someone had to die for that crime and poor Sudor was found guilty of first degree murder. Within a year he was executed and no more was said of the affair.

"Ronald Mansfield, you may be interested to learn, moved shortly thereafter to another state. He got his degree and in a while he published his first novel. He has been writing books and teaching philosophy ever since."

Several members of the party shifted uneasily in their chairs.

"Well, James, a very moral little tale. Pure balderdash, of course. My boy, I'm afraid you've been reading too many murder mysteries. Still, I seem to recall—you see, you'll have me reading them now as a result of your fairy tale!" There was a nervous quality to Professor Corneille's voice.

James Morley smiled at the silent gathering, threw down his drink and ran a pale hand through his hair. Within fifteen minutes the party broke up. Not a person could explain his sudden uneasiness.

But no one was very much surprised to hear the next morning that Professor James Morley had hanged himself, in the loneliness of his room.

The Blind Lady

"It is a great mystery to me," the old man said, "why you policemen always get so upset when justice is done." He creaked forward in his chair and grinned and patted Pearson's hand.

Pearson jerked the hand away. He tried to think of something really appropriate to say.

"Look at you now," the old man went on. "Dour, reproachful, scarcely touching your brandy—and excellent brandy it is, too, unless my memory is failing." He coughed. "Can't touch it, myself, you know. Which presents another problem: why is it, John, that when one grows old one is systematically denied all the necessities of life and granted all the luxuries?"

The big man with the flushed face brought his cigar back to life. "No one enjoys being shown up as a fool," he said.

"My dear friend, it is not necessary to be a fool to make a mistake!" Amos Carter chuckled and rubbed his cucumbery nose vigorously. "The difference between us, John," he said, "is that you must judge by externals, whereas I am not so obliged. That's all. But let's get on to other things; the merits of a system which every day sends men to prison on the weight of externals seems hardly worth an argument. There are pros and cons." He laughed. "I've made a joke. Pros and cons! Well, never mind. You are here for chess, not jokes or legal semantics."

Lieutenant John Pearson looked at the shriveled, spindly, fuzz-topped old man in the wheelchair and mused that such a bag of bones could be capable of stirring up so much trouble. Confined to the chair, half-paralyzed, Amos Carter hadn't set foot out of his crumbling brownstone for fifteen years; yet, because of him, because of this sneering, brilliant grandfather of grandfathers, the judicial system in America was becoming a laughing stock. And also because of Carter almost fifty convicted men and women—tried, convicted, sentenced to life imprisonment or, in some cases, the death house—were walking about the streets, restored citizens, free.

"Would you mind setting up the board?" The old man's eyes twinkled, danced; they said; Lieutenant Pearson, you are discomfited this evening. Is there a slight chance that this mood is in any way connected with the fact that your prize catch has been judged innocent of the crime for which you fought to have him executed? Could this be so?

They played quietly, evidently an even match for one another. Pearson finished his drink and accepted another and finished that one in less time than the first. His face began to glisten with perspiration.

"Do you *really* think the man is innocent?" he said, suddenly, in a loud voice.

Carter looked up and studied Pearson. "Passarelli?" he said, at last. "Of course he is innocent. Didn't I prove that beyond reasonable doubt?"

Pearson grunted. He thought of the wild-eyed guilty little man, and he remembered how the bodies had looked sprawled in the charred debris.

"You forget that one of the basic tenets of your club provides: Guilty until proven innocent; and that my approach is precisely the reverse. It has always been. That is why I formed my Court of Last Chance."

"How do you explain the fire, then?"

"I don't have to explain it. It isn't my concern. My concern was simply to prove that Santi Passarelli, appearances notwithstanding, in spite of all the evidence, did not start it." Carter smiled. "Your move, I believe."

"The fire was no accident."

"Then," Carter said unhesitatingly, "we are faced with the grim knowledge that the actual culprit is still at large. A matter which lies in *your* territory, not mine."

Lieutenant Pearson watched the old man carefully. Seated close to the hearth, swathed in layers of wool, Amos Carter did not manage to look the role of the Good Samaritan he played so noisily. Pearson wondered about the real motive; he'd long ago stopped believing it was an honest desire to see justice done. No; it seemed more an insane urge to get everybody out of jail, regardless, an urge sufficient to itself. Or perhaps it was a secret game the man played, a game whose reward was evenings like this, when he could gloat and mock and bask in his superior sun.

"You hate Passarelli, don't you?" the old man said, pleasantly.

Pearson gave the syllable organ depth and body: "Yes."

"Well, this will astound you, I suppose—but you know, I don't care for him, either. Disgusting little monkey; exactly the type who *would* set fire to a sanatorium. But ... it, remains that he is innocent of the crime. A pity, perhaps. You see, my particular kind of justice, like your own, is not always a matter for cheers—except in principle. Our Lady with the Scale is the same; mine peeks over her blindfold occasionally, that is all. It is still your move."

The snap of a burning log spat noise and specks of fire. Pearson loosened his collar. Strange thoughts began to occur to him. as brandy followed brandy.

What were the facts?

Santi Passarelli had been convicted on the testimony of witnesses who had seen him loitering about Hogarth Sanitarium. They had seen him wait until the fire was raging, then dash away. There was the fellow's record: a confirmed pyromaniac. Convicted and sent to prison in '37 for firing a candy factory in Chicago. Again in '43, an apartment unit. He had been in the neighborhood when the Golden Clover club burned down to the ground, killing over twenty people. There was the match test, the other tests. And finally there was his own confession— which, of course, he later denied. Judgment: not insane. A cold-blooded killer, ruthless, conscienceless, and now breathing free air that he had once polluted with the stink of burning flesh ...

"You see, lieutenant, you are handicapped," Carter said. "You go by appearances—which are seldom accurate. Take a golf ball. Show it to a Zulu native and the man would die and rot away before he'd ever guess the ball's insides to consist of a fibrous pulp. You read in the evening paper of a young scion who has kicked his mother to death and then berated her broken corpse with pointedly unfilial remarks. Immediately you hate the boy;

your jaws clamp, your fingers tighten. If he were to walk into the
same room, you would doubtless attack him. You do not realise
that the mother, bless her, had poisoned the boy's wife out of
jealousy, taken over the baby and then engineered to cheat her
son out of the inheritance left by his late father. The papers do
not tell you that, for the boy has decided not to tell the papers:
his fit of anger over, he retains a respect for his mother which
she had never shown him." Carter rubbed at his nose gleefully.
"Or, to take a more simple example," he continued: "Dog Kills
Tot. A big dog has chewed out the throat of its three-year-old
mistress. The public is shocked! The dog is put to death. Other
dogs are shut out of their homes. Of course, no one bothers to
look at the numerous scars and burnt spots on the first dog, the
hurtful sores that bear rather eloquent testimony to the sadistic
temperament of the young mistress. No one bothers to inquire
why the dog should have committed such an atrocity in the first
place." The old man gazed at a knight thoughtfully. "Appearances," he said.

Pearson pretended to be thinking about his move. Instead, he
thought about Santi Passarelli. How had Carter manipulated his
release? One by one, the witnesses had come forward and admitted that yes, they might have been mistaken. Yet, they'd been so
certain before! So positive! Olson, the star, confessed—and had
the papers to prove it—that he'd had a double abscess on his eye
and was therefore obliged to wear dark glasses, so he *could* have
been wrong. It might *not* have been Passarelli he'd seen . . .

And another strange thing: there was the surprise alibi, the
clincher, the mysterious figure who came out of hiding to swear
that Passarelli had been with him across the city on the night of
the fire. Come to think about it, in *most* instances—in the ones
where the freed parties were obviously, to Pearson, guilty—
there was this Mysterious Witness . . .

Pearson remembered Carter's bank account now. The old
man was swinishly rich, had been for years. He thought about
the strange transformation that takes place in otherwise upright
citizens at the sight of negotiable currency.

"By the way, John," Carter adjusted a muffler with his one

good hand, "I should have warned you—Mr. Passarelli tele-
phoned me last night. He's coming over later on this evening—to
thank me, I expect. I tried to prevent it, needless to say, but he
was—"

Pearson got to his feet quickly, the brandy racing through
him. His movement upset the chess table and this caused the
delicately carved pieces to scatter off to the floor. Automatically,
Carter propelled his chair backwards. The part of his face that
was not paralyzed twitched.

"Am I to understand you're conceding the game, Lieutenant?"
he said coldly.

Pearson's upper lip curled over his teeth. "Carter," he said,
making an effort to control his voice, "listen to me. You know
goddamn well that filthy little pig started the fire. You know it
as well as I do. You know Buchanan was guilty, too, You know
Shriker killed that kid. *Don't you?*" The big man stumbled only
slightly as he advanced toward the wheelchair.

Amos Carter smiled with half his face. His eyes seemed set on
pinwheels. "John Pearson, I do believe my brandy has gone to
your head. You're surely not suggesting that I've used my influence to assist those I do not genuinely—"

"When you started this Court of Last Chance I was with you—
remember that. Right down the line. Then your brain started to
get soft. You started springing losers. Losers like Schuh, like Phil
Janeway, the biggest narco pusher in this county. But even then,
Carter, even when I knew you were wrong, I was on your side
because I believed in what you were doing, I thought you did,
too. But you don't. You don't believe it at all." Pearson was leaning his hands on the arms of the wheelchair, his face inches away
from the old man's. "I don't know why you're doing it now. I'm
a cop, not a psychoanalyst. Maybe you have to be both; maybe
that's why I didn't peg you for a phony right off the bat. But
I'll tell you one thing now, and you'd better listen pretty damn
carefully. If that skunk Passarelli shows his miserable face in here
tonight I'll tear him into little pieces."

"That," Carter said, "would be one of your more serious mistakes."

Pearson pulled himself erect and looked down at the grinning old man. "When's he due?"

"He should have arrived twenty minutes ago."

Pearson looked at his watch. The numbers floated in his sight. He picked up the brandy bottle and then set it down again.

Amos Carter sighed. "I'm afraid, dear friend," he said, "that this marks a hiatus in a relationship which has been—or so I thought—of great mutual comfort. I judged incorrectly, I see; but that is merely another argument for my thesis on appearances. One would swear you were intelligent. You dress decently: no ventilated shoes, no trenchcoat; you play a fair game of chess ... well, *vogue la galère!* Pity it should happen now at this time, though. I was hoping to surprise you."

Pearson knotted his fingers, then he relaxed them and went to the couch where he picked up his coat and hat.

"Don't you even want to know the surprise?"

"Good night, Carter."

"Do you by any chance recall a certain Mrs. Feverell?"

Pearson paused. Gloria Feverell—yes, he remembered her. She'd been found guilty of having poisoned her husband one night. A stunning four-time widow.

"What about her?"

Carter's eyes were fierce brightnesses. "As a result of some correspondence and a little investigation," he said, "I am prepared to release definite proof that the unfortunate lady has been the victim of an enormous miscarriage of justice. She was at a motion picture at the time of the crime, you see. Good night, Lieutenant. You'd best hurry, or Mr. Passarelli will—"

Suddenly Amos Carter jerked his purple beak into the air and screamed.

His good hand flapped out like a pale wing.

Pearson tried to clear his mind. There had been a sound just before the scream: a sound like the popping of resin on a log.

Carter rolled his chair frantically, but as he could use only one hand, the chair came forward and then circled back again. "Help me!" the old man cried.

Pearson saw what had happened. When he'd upset the chess

table, Carter had moved his chair closer to the flaming hearth. Some fire had spit out and caught on his woolen shawls.

And now Amos Carter was on fire.

"Help me, in the name of God, John!"

Pearson took a step forward.

Then he stopped.

He thought of many things, all at once. They crowded his brain and caused his head to hurt.

The wheelchair was making frantic circles, around and around; it careened, waves of flame rising in excited plumes from the loosely woven cloth. The air was full of smoke and fire and screams.

Pearson watched the drapes catch, then the tapestries; he watched, holding his hands to his ears.

At last the cries stopped and the chair stopped.

Quietly the chair burned and the thing in it burned and there was suddenly an acrid aroma in the room.

It grew.

The big red-faced man stepped quietly outside into the shadows.

He put on his hat and waited and presently he heard the footsteps and presently he saw the face that belonged to the footsteps.

A dark small face, hairy, with small wild eyes.

Lieutenant Pearson smiled and took out his revolver.